FINDING HIS REDEMPTION

AN ENEMIES TO LOVERS ROCK STAR ROMANCE

MELANIE A. SMITH

WICKED DREAMS PUBLISHING

Kindle eBook ISBN: 978-1-952121-18-0
eBook ISBN: 978-1-952121-19-7
Paperback ISBN: 978-1-952121-20-3
Hardback ISBN: 978-1-952121-21-0

BOOKS BY MELANIE A. SMITH

The Safeguarded Heart Series

The Safeguarded Heart

All of Me

Never Forget

Her Dirty Secret

Recipes from the Heart: A Companion to the Safeguarded
Heart Series

The Safeguarded Heart Complete Series: All Five Books
and Exclusive Bonus Material

Standalone Romance Novels

Everybody Lies

Last Kiss Under the Mistletoe

Tough Love

Finding His Redemption

Life Lessons: A series that can be read as standalones

Never Date a Doctor

Bad Boys Don't Make Good Boyfriends

You Can't Buy Love

The Heart of Rutherford: Life Lessons Novels 1 – 3

Short Stories

Cruising for Love

CONTENTS

Chapter 1	1
Chapter 2	12
Chapter 3	24
Chapter 4	35
Chapter 5	46
Chapter 6	53
Chapter 7	58
Chapter 8	66
Chapter 9	79
Chapter 10	91
Chapter 11	106
Chapter 12	120
Chapter 13	136
Chapter 14	150
Chapter 15	161
Chapter 16	180
Chapter 17	186
Chapter 18	194
Chapter 19	202
Chapter 20	210
Chapter 21	216
Chapter 22	223
Chapter 23	231
Chapter 24	239
Chapter 25	246
Chapter 26	252
Chapter 27	263
Chapter 28	280
Epilogue	284

Acknowledgments 291
About the Author 293

1

Back in Black by AC/DC

West

"There is *nothing* more overrated than bacon, dude."

Andy, my driver, smirks at me in the rearview mirror. His light blue eyes are already mocking me. "Nope. I've got that beat: joining the mile high club. No contest."

"Are you serious? Look, everything is either wrapped in, flavored as, or made to look like bacon these days. It's ridiculous. But getting your rocks off at forty thousand feet? Well, that's just a good time, and in *no* way overrated. I don't know how you could even suggest that."

"Have you actually tried fucking someone in one of those tiny bathrooms? It isn't easy. Or fun. Or conducive to getting anyone off," he argues, one hand agitatedly running through his curly blond hair.

"Ever heard of private planes? Or the sin bin?" I counter. I watch with smug satisfaction as Andy's eyebrows jump in the mirror.

"First, private planes are some serious next-level celebrity shit, Mr. I'm Flying Commercial These Days." He gives me a pointed look, and I flip him off for going for a sore spot. "Second: What's a sin bin? Is that slang for doing it in the place they have those tiny flight attendant chairs? Because that's not exactly private and definitely a good way to get banned from ever flying again."

I chuckle. "A sin bin is this little bedroom they have over the main cabin on some airplanes so flight attendants can rest on long flights where they change shifts. I'll let you figure out why they call it a sin bin." I waggle my eyebrows.

"Again: Fucking a flight attendant falls under 'next-level celebrity shit.' I'm sticking to my guns. For us everyday Joes, joining the mile high club is the most overrated thing I can think of. Fight me."

"Well, since I'm clearly not back to private plane status, I'll use this opportunity flying *commercial* to prove you wrong."

Andy laughs and smacks the steering wheel. "Video or it didn't happen."

I shake my head. "Are you trying to get me in trouble? I'm supposed to be a saint now, remember? The last thing I need is a video out there of me fucking some rando on an airplane."

"Yeah, yeah, yeah," Andy grumbles jokingly. "Ruin all my fun, why don't you."

"Uh-huh. This whole conversation was just to bait me into doing something stupid, wasn't it?"

I'm teasing, really. I've known Andy for years, since before rehab, even, so I know he wouldn't do me like that.

"West. Bro. You know nobody has to bait you into doing something stupid. You do that just fine on your own. So as much as I'd like to hear your take on airplane bathroom sex, maybe you're right and you should just focus on behaving for a while."

"Now you're ruining all *my* fun. I just said there couldn't be a video." I give him a wink just as he pulls to a stop.

He shakes his head at me while he radios the guards. A few moments later there's a knock on the tinted window.

"That's my cue. Thanks for the ride, man."

"Be good, West. For all our sakes."

"Oh, I will. I'll be very, *very* good," I promise with a sly smile.

He flips me off and laughs as I step out into the hazy California sunshine. Two guards quickly flank me, one on either side, and I hand my backpack off to one. The other reaches for my guitar case, but I give him a look that says exactly how dead he'll be if he touches my Rosie. *Nobody* touches my girl.

I slip on my aviators, look around, and realize that I'm in the best mood I've been in for a while. I'm sober. The band is back together. Our album is climbing the charts. And I can feel people's eyes on me. That is what I lived through rehab for. What I've climbed back out of the pit I dug for myself for. The attention. The adoration. The rock and roll life. Icing on the cake that is my resuscitated music career.

Before we can even make it three steps, one brave soul, a dude who looks just a few years younger than me, darts around one of my huge guards and thrusts out a pen and notebook.

"Holy shit, you're Kristoffer Westberg! Can I have your autograph?"

A lazy grin spreads over my face and I signal the guards to stand down. "Sure, man, anything for a fan." I lean in and grab the pen, scrawling messily one-handed over the page. As soon as I'm done, the guy holds his cellphone up and I barely have time to throw up a peace sign before he snaps a pic. He releases me, turning to giddily show the pic to his friend, and I shake my head and laugh as we walk away.

We manage to make it the next twenty steps to the terminal without incident, but as soon as we're inside, the familiar gasps of recognition and cries of "West!" follow me. I keep my cool, looking straight ahead like it's no big deal. Happens every day. But damn does it feel good. Like coming home.

The guards start spreading their arms and taking up space, presumably to keep people away, and I soon know why as I pick up flashes in my peripheral vision. I wasn't aware the paparazzi had infiltrated SFO, but hey, bring it on. I'm going to have to deal with it at LAX soon anyway. And the band's album dropped recently enough that we can use all the attention we can get. Enjoying it? That's just a bonus.

I take my time strolling toward security, letting them follow, take pictures, and shout questions my PR people would kill me if I answered as my guards continue to push them back. I can see the guys at the checkpoint exchanging nervous glances, but the small crowd of photographers and onlookers drops back — well, are pushed back by my guards — as I lift my guitar case and lay it lovingly on the conveyor belt, followed by a bin that I unceremoniously dump my wallet, keys, jacket, and shoes into.

As I make it through, followed quickly by my bodyguards, murmurs start back up, but nothing like what they were before. No more paps. And no one else approaches, even though I can hear the whispers. Like music to my ears after the quiet halls of the "wellness center" I spent far too long cooped up in to get back to this place. And by this place, I don't mean heading home to L.A. — I mean this place where I've gotten back my freedom, fans, and fame.

The rest of the walk to the gate and the boarding process are uneventful, save a flirty look from the chick at the boarding door. But the cute brunette flight attendant who greets me gives me a smile that says she knows exactly who I am. She manages to help me stow Rosie in the first-class closet and seat me without fangirling. Points for professionalism. But she won't be so professional later when I'm fucking her in the lavatory I passed on my way in. A shit-eating grin spreads over my face. I may or may not actually do it, but thinking about it is fun either way.

I don't make eye contact with the dude in the seat next to mine as I slump down and pop my earbuds in, sending the universal "fuck off" signal. He doesn't look like he'd be a fan with his pressed khakis and pristine polo shirt, and I'm certainly not looking to fuck him in a bathroom. The thought makes me chuckle.

The plane pushes back from the gate and gets into the air without event. When the same brunette flight attendant comes around to take our drink orders, I pause my music but leave the earbuds in.

"Mr. Marshall," she says to the dude next to me. "Nice to see you. I presume you'd like your usual vodka tonic?"

I can't help it, I raise an eyebrow and turn to look at the guy. Surprisingly, he looks sidelong at me and shakes his head. "Just a Sprite is fine, Mandy, thank you."

That gets my attention. Mostly because it's said in the exact tone I hear all the time. The one people use when they know they're within earshot of an alcoholic. Great.

"Oh," she says, sounding surprised. "Well, all right then." She turns to me, and I politely pop my earbuds out. "And what can I get for you?"

"Just ice water, thanks," I mumble self-consciously.

She moves on, but I can still feel Sprite guy's eyes on me. I pull off my aviators — that were clearly fooling no one — and run my fingers through my messy dark brown hair. I glance over at him and he smiles, offering a hand.

"I'm Morgan," he says pleasantly.

"Marshall, huh?" I reply, shaking his hand.

He chuckles. "Not *that* Marshall."

That gets a wry smile out of me. Maybe he does know who I am. Though I didn't really think he'd be related to the family that founded the amp manufacturing company. But you never know.

"Well, Morgan not-*that*-Marshall, I'm Kristoffer Westberg."

"So, what do I call you? Kristoffer? Kris? Or do you actually prefer West?" he muses.

I huff a short laugh. Yep. He knows.

"West is fine," I reply.

"Cool," he replies, nodding slowly. "You know, my sister is going to shit a brick when I tell her I met you."

That gets a chuckle out of me. "Well, if you have something I can sign, I'm always happy to autograph something for a fan."

Morgan considers me for a moment. "Thanks, but I wouldn't say she's a fan. Though she used to be your *biggest* fan. That was back in the day though."

Well fuck, that's got my attention.

"Used to be?"

Flight attendant Mandy returns with our drinks, and it just goes to show how distracted I am by Morgan's statement that I don't respond to the coy look she gives me. Instead, I watch Morgan pause to take a sip of his Sprite.

"Yep," he finally replies, smacking his lips on the "p" like a pompous ass. But he doesn't elaborate.

And I'm too fucking curious for my own good.

"So, what happened?"

The dude shrugs. "It's not my story to tell. But if you really want to know, she's a journalist at *Rock Scene Magazine* in L.A. now. You should go ask her." He reaches into the briefcase tucked against the wall of the plane at his feet and fishes out a business card.

I take the card, examining it curiously. *Max Marshall, Writer* is printed neatly over the magazine's logo, under which is an email address, phone number, and address downtown. It's a publication I've never heard of, but there are so many these days.

"Thanks," I murmur, still contemplating the little white rectangle. Wondering what turned Max Marshall off so much she went from my "biggest fan" to not one at all. Especially since she obviously hasn't lost her love of rock itself. The knowledge irks me more than I'd like to admit.

"Don't thank me yet," Morgan replies. I look up at the tone of his voice to find him smirking at me.

"Why not?" I ask warily.

Morgan tilts his head. "Because my sister brooks no bullshit. So don't ask if you don't want an honest answer. I mean, don't get me wrong, *I* think you guys are awesome. Max, on the other hand … anyway, just a fair warning."

I flip the card nervously as I think about his implication. She must really hate me. And I'm as annoyed by it as I am nervous. Sure, I fucked up, but that's in the past. I've paid my dues. The band's back and better than ever. So what's her damage? What can she possibly hold against me now?

I look back up at Morgan Marshall, who is now buried in his laptop screen with some serious "fuck off" vibes of his own going on. Obviously he's not in the mood for any further discussion on the topic. I'm so twisted up by the idea of Max Marshall and her story that I don't even try to fuck the hot flight attendant. Probably for the best since it's a short flight anyway.

I do try to chat up Morgan as we're waiting for the door to open, but he pointedly sticks to polite, superficial chatter. He's a software engineer who works in both the San Francisco Bay Area and Los Angeles, though he's based in L.A. He loves our new album and wants to know when the tour is. That's where I have to be vague and dodgy because it hasn't been announced yet. And after that we're disembarking, and I lose him as soon as I'm joined by my L.A. security and start pushing through the waiting crowd.

Probably best we didn't talk more about his sister.

I want to hear it straight from the horse's mouth anyway. If there was ever a time to make sure every media outlet is on our side, right before announcing our comeback tour is it.

Guess it's time to pay a visit to *Rock Scene Magazine*.

2

Everybody Loves Me by OneRepublic

Max

"I'm sorry, can you repeat that?" I ask my assistant blankly.

"Kristoffer Westberg is here to see you," she whispers again, this time glancing over her shoulder.

"Did he say *why*?" I reply, looking into the main office area to make sure he didn't follow her from reception.

Rock stars like Kristoffer Westberg don't just drop by the office of a small, albeit well-established, industry magazine. Especially not specifically asking for a reporter who long ago stopped giving a shit about him and his band.

Alexsis screws her lips to the side and shakes her head. I refrain from getting on her case for not asking. But I can tell by the waves of nervous excitement coming off of her that the dark good looks and charisma that I'm all too familiar with have had their way with her tender, young heart. *Been there, sister.*

I rise with a sigh, putting my best polite face on. Alexsis fidgets nervously behind me as I step out from behind my high cubicle walls into the open-plan main office area.

And lo and behold, there he is, leaning casually against the wall next to the reception desk, somehow managing to look bored and above it all yet totally charming at the same time. The asshole.

He straightens up when he catches sight of us approaching, and my mind vaults back three years to the last time I saw him. Just as smoldering hot. Just as intimidating, even at only a couple inches over my five-foot-eight self. Same thick, dark eyebrows set over equally dark eyes. Same straight nose and defined jawline with just a bit of stubble. Same tight black T-shirt and dark-wash jeans. I guess when a look works for you, you stick with it. And I must admit — albeit begrudgingly —the look works for him at thirty-six just as much as it did at twenty-two. Possibly more.

What's different is that his dark eyes are much

clearer this time as they rake over my Rolling Stones T-shirt and ripped black skinny jeans down to my black Doc Martens.

I stop in front of him and raise an eyebrow. "Mr. Westberg. What an unexpected surprise."

His eyes flick up to mine and his trademark too-cool-for-school grin slides onto his stupidly handsome face. And despite myself, more than a decade of being infatuated with this man can't be wiped away by a few years of disgust, as something deep in my chest twinges at his gaze. Christ.

"*You're* Max Marshall?" he asks with an incredulous note to his rough voice.

Both eyebrows rise to my hairline. "Expecting a man?" I taunt.

I take note of Alexsis slinking into the receptionist's chair and resting her chin on her hands to watch the show.

"Nope," he replies. "I met your brother on a flight last weekend." He holds up something I immediately recognize as my business card. "He said I should talk to you. But he didn't say you were…" He trails off, his eyes roaming intently over my body. "So young."

I fight back a scoff, knowing that is almost certainly *not* what he was thinking. And at thirty-one, I wouldn't exactly call myself young. Well, not compared to him at least.

"Yes, well, he also didn't bother mentioning to me that you were coming, so I apologize for the less-than-stellar welcome." I have to fight to keep the sarcasm and annoyance out of my voice both at my brother for sending this douche canoe my way knowing how I feel about him, and at West himself for living up to the creep he is in my head. "Is there something you wanted to discuss with me in particular, or is there something *Rock Scene* can do for the band? If the latter, I can have one of my colleagues —"

West shakes his head, his dark eyes glittering in a way that makes me more than a little uncomfortable. Like he knows a joke I'm not in on.

"No, I'm here for you. Is there someplace we can talk?"

That stupid traitor feeling in my chest twists again. Oh, how younger me would've once loved to hear those words come out of that mouth. I grind my teeth together in frustration as I mentally weigh how I want to deal with him.

"Yes, fine," I eventually say with exasperation. "Follow me."

I turn and catch Alexsis's expression of curiosity and shoot her a "don't even think about eavesdropping" look as I lead West through the office.

For good measure, I pass by my cubicle in favor of the conference room in the back corner. It almost never gets used, especially not at the end of a Friday afternoon.

He saunters by me into the small room, and when I turn back from closing the door, he's sprawled in the chair at the head of the six-person table. I take a seat pointedly on the other end.

With a grin, he leans forward on his elbows, his toned biceps flexing under the hem of his shirtsleeves. I look away, at the wall. Anywhere but at those arms.

"Morgan said you didn't like me. Clearly he wasn't exaggerating."

I drag my eyes back to him and lean forward on my elbows, giving him a challenging look. "My brother said that, did he?"

West's grin fades into a smirk. "Well, sort of. He said you 'used to be my biggest fan,'" he replies, using air quotes.

I can't help it; a wry laugh escapes me.

"Well, tell me how you really feel," he jokes with a smirk.

"Oh, you really don't want me to do that," I assure him.

He cocks an eyebrow.

"Maybe that's exactly what I want you to do."

I lift an eyebrow in return. "Maybe you should tell me what you wanted."

"This is what I wanted."

"You wanted to know why I'm not your biggest fan anymore?" I ask with undisguised incredulity.

West's chin dips in agreement, and I have to admit that I'm more than a little shocked.

"I'm not sure I'm comfortable having this discussion here." Read: *Are you trying to get me fired, asshole?* How can I sit in the office of the rock and roll magazine I've dedicated my career to and bad-mouth one of the biggest rock stars of my generation? As low as my brain-to-mouth filter usually is, even I know nothing good can come of it.

West's eyes capture mine and my palms start to sweat under the scrutiny, nerves seizing my whole body.

"Come on. Tell me why you don't like me anymore," he pleads with an affected pout.

I swallow hard against the lump in my throat. "Why does it matter?"

"It just does," he replies in a deceptively nonchalant tone.

But he wouldn't be asking if it didn't matter. A lot. This is surreal.

I rub my lips together, deciding what answer won't jeopardize my job. But then I realize I don't owe Kristoffer Westberg a goddamn thing, including the truth. So I just stare at him for a minute, hoping he'll let it go.

After a few beats, he looks down, shaking his head, and says seemingly to himself, "She's lost that lovin' feelin'."

My eyes go wide as he stands and heads purposely toward me. And as he drops to one knee beside me, I realize exactly what he's about to do. He's about to go full *Top Gun* on my ass. Right here. Right now. Fuuu-uuuckkkkk.

Just as he starts belting out *You've Lost That Lovin' Feelin'* by the Righteous Brothers, I lunge forward and slam my hand over his mouth before the whole office hears and comes running.

"Are you insane?!"

He grabs my hand and rises, pulling me with him all in one swift motion, and I abruptly notice the electric zap that crawls up my arm from where he's touching me and how *close* he is. How good he smells. Like cologne and cool night air and guitar strings. So much better than the last time we were this close, when he smelled like booze and weed and heartbreak. But smelling of it or not, West is a whole lot of heartbreak waiting to happen.

At the thought, I pull my hand back abruptly.

"Worked for Maverick," he says with a shrug, his eyes searching my face. "You really don't want to tell me what your deal is, do you?"

I lift my chin stubbornly in answer.

"Come on," he pleads winningly. "I'm all better now. Don't you want to jump back on the West train?"

I pull a face. "Don't you mean the Violent Mood Swings train?" And then I think silently to myself, *You know, your band, you self-centered ass hat?*

"Sure, yeah, that too," he agrees dismissively.

I sigh heavily. "Not for all the guitar picks in a Dunlop factory."

"Ouch, Maxi. Ouch."

I frown. "It's Max."

West grins. "Okay, Maxi. Whatever you say."

"You know, annoying the shit out of me isn't going to make me tell you," I snap at him. Even though I'm more mad that I actually find his bullshit kind of cute. His mischievous grin shows that dimple in his right cheek, and his behavior is a heady combination of endearing and playful. Dear god, help me. I take a step back, needing to distance myself in every way possible.

"Then forget why. I'm all better now. Don't you want to give me another chance?" he cajoles, leaning back against the wall and looking like a butt-hurt little kid.

"Yes, well, that's great, but just because you're magically all better doesn't change the way I feel. But really, good luck with the album and tour and stuff."

"Who said anything about a tour?" he asks slyly.

I narrow my eyes at him. "You guys aren't going to tour?"

"Yeah, of course we're going to tour. But nobody's said anything about one yet."

I throw my hands up. "Do you ever take anything seriously?"

"Absolutely. Music. Rosie. And why you're so mad at me."

I shake my head. "I can't believe you named your guitar after an AC/DC song," I grumble.

"How did you know that? I've never actually said that publicly," he says, squinting at me like he thinks I might be a stalker.

No need to tell him I flirted heavily with the line between groupie and just that once upon a time.

"It wasn't obvious?" I ask innocently, batting my eyelashes.

"Okay, fine. But don't think I don't know deflecting when I hear it. I'm the goddamn king of it, Maxi." He steps forward back into my space. "And maybe I need you back on board. Seriously." My brain goes numb for a minute as he stares down at me intently. And I *almost* forget everything he's done. Such is the magic of Kristoffer Westberg. "What's it going to take?"

I blink hard. "For me to forgive and forget?"

"Yes."

"You could try apologizing." I step back and frown. "But then, you owe that to a whole lot more people than me. More important people."

West's answering frown mimics my own. "Like who?"

He asks it like he's never even considered that he might need to apologize for the epic failure he was to his fans. Alcohol. Drugs. Arrests. More drugs. Breaking up the best goddamn band of my formative years. I'm the least of those he's hurt. And I know I'm not the only one who has no interest in his supposed reformation. In fact, judging by the album's weak sales, I'm in the majority.

All things I don't say. If he doesn't know, it's not my job to clue him in. And I don't think he'd listen anyway. He seems to think all should automatically be forgiven.

He continues to stare at me expectantly.

I take a deep breath. "Like your fans, for starters."

His expression darkens. "I went to rehab. Got the band back together. Put out a new album. That's not enough?"

I laugh ironically. Partly because he's just confirmed my exact thought about him. But mostly...

"What?" he asks in an uncharacteristically snappish tone, interrupting my train of thought.

"It's just funny. Because your comeback album is titled *Redemption*."

"So?"

I stare at him. He can't be serious. But I know he is. Poor, clueless fallen rock star.

"You don't get redemption without forgiveness. For which you need to both express regret *and* make up for it." I know I've lost him before he even replies.

"Meaning?"

"Meaning you think you've made it up to the fans, but you haven't expressed regret for the things you've done. Not publicly at least." His brows scrunch together, and I sigh knowing he just doesn't get it. "You need to apologize, West. And it needs to be big."

He scoffs. "And look like a pussy? I think my actions speak loudly enough. The album is doing just fine, after all. The fans are coming back."

I don't bother disagreeing with him.

"Then why are you here? You can't possibly expect everybody to love you. Why bother tracking down one silly little reporter who isn't a fan anymore?" I point out.

He steps back. "You know what? You're right. I don't know why I bothered coming here. All the people who matter are on my side. Have a nice life, Maxi."

He gives me a mocking salute. And then he leaves.

I'd laugh at his stubborn ass, but it's too sad. Because I know I'm going to be living rent-free in Kristoffer Westberg's self-absorbed brain as he struggles with the fact that not everybody loves him like he thinks they do. And as disappointed as I've been by him, I feel for the struggle he has coming. Because you can't fix something you don't think is broken.

3

Welcome to the Jungle by Guns N' Roses

West

"You're late, West."

"You're an asshole, Ward."

"Why don't you guys just fuck each other already?" Nik suggests.

I shoot her a comically lecherous look. "I think you mean, why don't I just fuck you already?"

I'm only half-joking. Nikka Jones, with her bright green hair, tiny mouthful titties, and tight ass, is definitely fuckable.

She snorts. "Even if I could stomach the thought of having a dick inside me, I'm pretty sure my girlfriend couldn't."

"Well, then you and Ward are both out of luck. Because if I haven't fucked him in the last eighteen years, I'm sure as hell not about to start now."

Ward smirks at me from across the rehearsal space and, all joking aside, I'm happy to let him bust my chops. Because Ward Pierce is the best, and oldest, friend I've got. We met and formed Violent Mood Swings when we were eighteen. Half our lives ago. But as good-looking as the dude is with his height, blond hair, and sweet tats, I just don't swing that way. Not even for one of the best lead singers of all time; seriously, dude's got a voice that has melted panties worldwide. Probably better for the band that I don't. We would've broken up even sooner and never gotten back together, given my relationship track record. And I use the term "relationship" loosely.

"All right, ladies," James, our only other remaining founding member, and the total dad of the group — seeing as how he's the only actual dad — chides us from behind the keyboards. "Can we rehearse or what? Some of us have families to get home to."

Michael holds up a drumstick in silent agreement. I snort. Because Michael lives with his parents. I can't give him shit for that though, even though he's twenty-eight, since he just came off a bad divorce.

"Yeah, yeah, whatever, bitches," I grumble,

pulling Rosie out of her velvet-lined case. The vintage cherry Gibson SG Standard beauty was the first luxury I ever allowed myself once we hit it big all those years ago. And she's been my number one girl ever since. The only steady woman in my life. I tune up and watch Ward do his mic check.

Rehearsal goes fucking perfect, and even Ward, with his seemingly never-ending nit-picking is confident that we're ready to tour. But then, he should be: He wrote most of the songs and has made us rehearse more for this tour than all of our past ones combined.

He pulls me aside once James and Michael have headed out and Nik is packing up her bass.

"You were on today."

I finish locking my guitar case and look up at him. And if I couldn't tell by his tone of voice, the scrutinizing look pretty much says it all.

"Why don't you tell me what you really want to say?"

I plop down on the battered leather couch against the wall and pat the cushion next to me.

He sits down, folding a leg under him.

"You've been a little distracted lately. And you were late this morning."

"Still not a question," I point out with a tired smile.

"Don't bullshit me."

I roll my head toward him and look him in the eye.

"I can't stop thinking about that stupid fucking reporter."

"What does the reporter have to do with you being late?"

I grimace. "I couldn't sleep."

"Shit, dude, jerk off like the rest of us and get some shut-eye next time."

I roll my eyes at him. "I wasn't thinking about her like *that*." I shudder for effect. Trying to ignore the fact that she *is* objectively hot, with her long wavy brown hair, hazel eyes, cute button nose, pink bow lips, and tits and curves for days. But I still hate her. "It just gets me. Who the fuck is she to not forgive me? She obviously liked our music. Isn't the music what matters?"

"What's the Abraham Lincoln quote? You can please all of the people some of the time, some of the people all of the time —"

"Yeah, yeah, yeah. You can't please all of the people all of the time. I know. We've just worked so fucking hard, man. What if she's right? What if the fans don't show up like we think they will?"

Ward is one of the only people on the planet I'd admit my fears to. But even saying it out loud freaks me out on a level I'm not fully capable of dealing with. I went through hellfire to get here, and it can't be for nothing.

"I'm going to be honest with you, man." He scrubs a hand over the back of his neck. "I haven't paid attention to sales. Like at all. I'm not here for the fans. I'm here for the music. If the fans come back, great. If they don't, fine. We've come so far. You've come so far. I'm actually just really proud of our progress, and you should be too."

A sigh escapes me. Because I wish I were as confident as Ward. Deep down though, I'm just not. I need the validation. But like fuck I'm going to admit *that* out loud. Even to Ward. Just admitting it to myself just shows how much good all the damn head-shrinking I had in rehab did. But baby steps. Admitting it to myself is hard enough. Let's not go too crazy and start talking about this shit out loud like we're a couple of chicks or something.

"You know I'm all about the fans," I reply. "I'm just worried that we're doing all of this for nothing."

Ward waves a hand. "Do what you do best, man. Be happy with your effort, with how far you've come. That's what matters most," he reiterates.

"You're very zen today." I pull my head back and look at him. "You're not smoking weed again, are you?"

He laughs. "Hell no, dude. Los Angeles may be

the same old jungle, but you're not the only one who's changed. I'm high on life. You should be too. We're getting paid to do what we love again. The rest will come in time, I promise."

I stomp my feet dramatically. "But I want it noooooooow." It's my best Veruca Salt impression — the Willy Wonka movie one, not the alternative rock band — whining and all.

It gets a laugh out of Ward, which is what I was going for.

"Well, to be fair we have been playing it kind of safe. Since Nik and Michael are new and all. But I know the fans are important to you." Ward considers me for a moment. "We could up the stakes. Get some more attention."

I sit up, suddenly very interested. "Like how?"

"You could sing that song you wrote."

My face falls. "You know I can't do that."

"And you know it would be a game changer. You're good. Plus it's something new. Something different."

I shake my head emphatically. "Not gonna happen."

"But West —"

"Drop it."

Ward grimaces. "Fine. Guess you'll just have to humble yourself to the fans then."

"Just because some reporter at some nothing magazine says I need to apologize —"

Ward holds up his hands in surrender. "Fine, okay. Forget I said anything."

"Oh, I wi—"

"Reporter?" A sharp voice cuts in from the door.

We glance up to find our stout band manager filling the doorway, fixing us with a stern look. Or maybe that's just his face. Burke McKinley is one of the best in the business for a reason: He's a no-nonsense hard-ass, but he also gets shit done for his acts.

"Shit," I exclaim. "Sorry, Burke, didn't know you were here."

"Clearly," he says curtly. "What's this about a reporter?"

I roll my eyes and groan, sinking deeper into the couch like the rebellious teenager who still very much lives in my brain.

Ward shakes his head at me. "Some chick who writes for a rag called *Rock Scene*. She used to be West's 'biggest fan'" — Wade uses a cutesy voice that makes me glare at him — "but apparently thinks he needs to formally apologize for his piss-poor behavior."

Burke's eyebrows jump so high they nearly hit his receding hairline. He steps inside and shuts the door, grabbing a black metal folding chair from the stack against the wall and setting it backward in front of the couch. He sits down, straddling it to face us.

"I know that magazine. Small but well-respected." He taps his chin thoughtfully. "You know, she may be on to something."

I give him a disbelieving look, but he holds up a hand.

"Hear me out. It's been a while since you've interacted with the fans directly, at least publicly. And if we're going to tour, it can't hurt to get all the good press we can. So how about an apology tour? You go around apologizing, kissing babies, holding puppies, that sort of shit?"

I lean forward on my arms to respond, but Ward beats me to the punch.

"He's a musician, not a politician. That's ridiculous."

Burke narrows his eyes at Ward. "You think they don't do that for good reason? Image, son. It's all about image."

"We're a *hard rock band*," I cut in. "Isn't that kind of the exact opposite of the image we're going for? I mean, rock stars bite the heads off bats and kill chickens on stage —"

"Dude, that last one wasn't the band, that was the audience," Ward points out.

I roll my eyes. "You get my point though. We're not all babies and puppies and 'I'm so sorry for succumbing to the rampant sex, drugs, and alcohol that pervade the industry.'"

"Kristoffer," Burke starts in his best dad voice, "if there's a reporter out there willing to say it to your face, there are a hundred who aren't. I think it's the conservative approach to take this seriously."

Ward and I exchange unimpressed looks. I turn back to Burke.

"If I took everything reporters have said about me seriously, I would've offed myself by now," I reply. "But look. I get what you're saying. Image. Press opportunities. We can do that. How about 'Win a Date With West?' Or something like that. Something the fans really *want*."

Ward groans and rolls his eyes so hard I whack him on the back of the head.

"Come on, man," he laughs. "You have to admit that was a pretty douchey suggestion."

"And backwards," Burke adds. "You have to create desire before you fulfill it."

"Fine. What do you propose, then?" Ward counters.

"I'm hearing you," Burke assures us. "No babies. No puppies. But I think this apology idea could work. It plays on people's sympathies." He glances at me.

"And you can be charismatic when you want to. Work that to your advantage. Make *sure* the fans are back on board ahead of the tour announcement. It can't hurt album sales either, and we've got to start hyping any way we can ahead of the tour."

I purse my lips, trying not to give in just because he's using his best attempt at flattery. I do love some good flattery.

"Would it really be that bad?" Ward asks me directly.

I shoot an annoyed sidelong glance at him. "Not for you," I point out.

"One way or the other, I'm talking to PR about this. So what's it gonna take to get you on board, kid?" Burke asks flatly.

I throw up my hands. Burke is like a dog with a bone when he latches onto something. Goddamn Maxi Marshall and her stupid grudge.

Maxi Marshall. That's it.

"I want the reporter who suggested the idea to be there the whole time."

I ask knowing she'll never agree to it. There's my out.

Burke looks impressed. "That's fucking brilliant. I love it." I didn't mean it to be brilliant, but hey, two birds, one stone. "I'll get with Ford and we'll make it happen." He rises. "Oh, and I heard you guys practicing from my office. Sounding good. We're going to nail this tour, guys, you'll see."

He absently waves over his shoulder as he leaves, and I'm still silently absorbing what the fuck just happened. After a couple of minutes of silence, I look over at Ward.

"What the hell did I just sign up for?" I lament.

Ward snorts. "A public flogging led by a reporter who hates you?"

I groan and slump backward into the cushions.

"I'm so fucked."

Ward laughs and sinks next to me, patting me on the leg.

"Yes. Yes, you are. And not in the good way, either."

4

Don't Make Me Do It by Huey Lewis and the News

Max

"No."

"No?"

"I'm sorry, did I stutter? N. O. No."

"I'm sorry, did you forget that I'm your boss?"

I glare across the messy blue metal desk at Jason. "Did you forget how much I hate Kristoffer Westberg?"

"Can't you just get over it? At least enough to do this project?" he presses.

I smush my lips together. I haven't told him about West's visit. I didn't think he needed to know. But now …

"I … there's something you should know." Jason looks at me expectantly. "He came here last week." I give him the quick rundown on why he came and what was said. The highlights, anyway.

"Shit." Jason leans back in his chair.

"Yeah."

His dark eyes flick back up to meet mine. "I still need you to do this."

"Even though he's basically stalking me now?" I retort hotly.

He glances nervously at his office door. "You know they're going to be here any minute. I already told his manager you'd do it."

My jaw drops. "You did *not*," I gasp.

Jason levels a look at me. "I did. Because I'm. Your. Boss. This is *huge*, Max. Just what we need to raise our profile and attract new readers. We couldn't say no."

"But why meeeeeee?" I whine.

Jason runs a hand through his inky hair, his eyes soft and apologetic.

"The deal was contingent on your involvement." I start to protest but he holds up a hand "Don't worry. They are hiring you for a professional project, as a representative of *Rock Scene*. I'll make sure everything is on the up and up. You're not going to be stalked by a rock star on my watch." He smirks playfully.

I fold my arms over my chest and try my hardest not to pout. "Yeah, we'll see about that. So exactly what kind of professional project are we talking here?"

"We'll find out in —" he checks his watch. "Well, anytime now. They're late."

Figures. I groan and let my head slump down onto the close edge of his desk. I take a deep breath and sit back up. Then I take a moment to mentally put my big girl panties on.

"I'll hear what they have to say. That's all I can promise right now." Wow, that even sounded convincing to me.

Jason's relief is obvious. "Good. Let's go get set up then."

He rises and opens the door, gesturing for me to precede him out with an encouraging look. I roll my eyes and walk, huffing all the way down the hall to the conference room. Pointedly *not* stopping at my cubicle for something to take notes with. I know I'm being childish, but I find myself unable to stop.

Jason says nothing about my lack of preparedness, but before we can make it to the room, Ashley, our receptionist, intercepts us.

"They're here," she whispers to Jason like West

and his posse are going to hear us all the way across the building. I refrain from rolling my eyes at the reverent wonder in her voice. I've already rolled them about a thousand times in the last ten minutes. Wouldn't want them to pop out. Jason, on the other hand, responds by following her back to her desk.

I head into the conference room to give myself another minute to prepare. I choose the same seat as last time, at the foot of the table. I've barely begun to contemplate all the ways this could go wrong when I hear multiple voices, including Jason's, approaching.

My insides tumble as four men file into the room. Jason, West, Burke McKinley — a broad, short man with little hair and lots of presence whom I've never met but would have to live under a rock not to recognize — and a fourth guy who looks way too young to be invited to this party.

I rise from my chair and slap on the least-fake smile I can muster.

Until my eyes connect with West's as Jason and the other two men talk. He winks at me nonchalantly, and my smile melts into surprise as a jolt runs through my body like he just threw a live wire at me. He holds my gaze until I hear Jason introducing me.

"And this is my best and brightest, Max Marshall," Jason says, gesturing toward me as he steps around West to allow everyone comfortably into the room.

I catch a small smirk on West's lips as I force myself to look away.

"Gentlemen," I greet them.

The younger one who I don't know steps forward and offers a hand. Up close he looks not a day over twenty-five, is around West's height, and has light brown hair and blue eyes. He's not bad looking.

"Ms. Marshall, I'm Ford Nelson, West's public relations manager," he greets me importantly.

I watch West roll his eyes as he slumps into the chair behind Ford. My eyes flick back to Ford, mentally banking the fact that West clearly does not like Ford. Suddenly I find Mr. Nelson quite intriguing.

"A pleasure," I reply sweetly. My eyes move to Burke McKinley, who is settling into the chair across the table from West. "And Mr. McKinley, it's an honor to meet you."

"Call me Burke," he responds gruffly, sliding a piece of paper each to Jason, at the head of the table, and me. "And sign these while you're at it."

I glance down at the page. It's a nondisclosure agreement. My eyes flick up to Mr. McKinley's — Burke's — but it's Ford who pipes up.

"Standard NDAs. The lawyers won't even let us talk until you sign, I'm afraid."

Jason signs without hesitation. I, however, actually read it. Thankfully, it's not long. And Ford wasn't lying, it is all pretty standard. No disclosing anything we're not permitted to for the rest of our lives or they take everything we own and make us pariahs in the industry, blah blah blah. The usual. The ink hasn't even dried on my signature when Burke reaches out and whisks it away.

"So," he puffs. "It's actually thanks to your idea, Ms. Marshall, that we're here today."

I cock an eyebrow. "It's Max. And I'm sorry, did you say *my* idea?"

West is tracing circles on the table with a finger, but I don't miss the small smile at my question.

"I did," Burke affirms. "You suggested it would be prudent for West to apologize publicly. And that's exactly what we plan to do. A series of apologies, actually. An apology tour, as it were."

Whatever I was expecting to hear, it sure as shit wasn't that. They're turning his repentance into a fucking PR opportunity. Awesome. I don't know how they think this will work, but real remorse can't be choreographed.

"I'm still not quite sure I understand," I admit. "A tour? Like he's going to go to cities around the world and apologize to the fans? Like, that's it? And I, what, document it all?"

"We were thinking something more focused. Pre-chosen people or groups of people. We haven't nailed that part down yet, but the vision is to format it something like a reality TV program."

"We don't do extended video pieces. A few minutes here or there for interviews, but we're no production company," Jason interjects.

"We have a production company in mind for that part. What we need is someone to host, after a fashion," Burke explains. "Someone to go with West on a series of prearranged visits, to ask him questions before and after, then to document it in a multipage spread and online article that will go live at the same time as the finished video piece." He holds his hands up like he's writing a billboard. "West's Road to Redemption."

A snort escapes before I can stop it.

West sighs and looks up at the ceiling.

Ford raises a brow. "You don't like it?"

I press my lips together and shrug. "I just … I don't think I'm your girl."

"You're our girl because West says you are," Burke says flatly. "You're a reporter, aren't you? That's all this is. Reporting on a tour."

I shouldn't be surprised in the least that it was West particularly who brought me into this. Payback for not bowing and scraping, I suppose. And I don't bother correcting him that I'm not a reporter, I'm a journalist. I doubt he cares about the difference, even if I do.

I lean forward, knitting my fingers together as I choose my words. Finally, I look up, between Burke and Ford. "I presume you want everything done in a light favorable to West. Which is why I'm telling you: I'm not your girl."

A sly smile unfurls on Ford's face. "Ah, but that's the catch. We want honesty. Well, to a point. On the tour especially, we *want* someone who will ask the difficult, real questions. We're looking for raw moments that will capture the fans. Mind, they'll be edited later to ensure the desired effect, of course. And the article … well, maybe a little softer there, but no less honest. Though not *un*favorable. The idea is to show enough of the man he is in the fans' eyes trying to become the man they want him to be. And by the end, we really want to get the fans feeling that he's changed. Do you think you can work within those terms?"

Do I think I can contribute to deceiving fans into thinking any of the bullshit they orchestrate is reality? That West has really changed when I'm not convinced he has? My eyes land on West, who has returned to messing with the table. But like he feels my gaze, his eyes snap up to meet mine.

"I can't control what you edit to make things appear the way you want, but I also can't participate in something that's all for show," I say to Ford while keeping my eyes on West. Then I tip my head to West. "Are you going to really do this?"

West tilts his head to the side and his brows pinch together.

"Why else would I be here?" His first words since he showed up.

Despite their surface meaning, his words don't sit right with me. I give him a long, hard look and he smirks back at me. It just underscores my sense that West still has a long way to go before he's ready to earn that redemption he thinks he's entitled to.

"I'm not sure that I can," I admit, tearing my gaze from West to meet Ford's eyes. The disapproval there is obvious.

I glance over at Jason, who has been suspiciously quiet this whole time. All he does is shrug. Great. Guess I'm on my own.

"Let's reframe," Ford offers. "The current plan is to announce the album tour at the end of next month. How successful do you think ticket sales will be, Max?"

I give him a funny look. "What the hell do I know about ticket sales?"

"I think you know what I'm really asking," Ford insists.

I purse my lips. Ah. Yes. Yes, I guess I do know what he's really asking. The same thing West was asking the first time he showed up here.

With a heavy sigh, I decide not to shy away from the truth this time. "I'd noticed album sales were weak, and I wasn't surprised. Not because the album isn't good. It is, actually. But because, like me, I think a lot of people aren't willing to overlook the past. West burned a lot of fans with his actions. The cancelled concerts. Showing up so stoned off his ass he could barely play. The end was rough enough, even without the little public incident that landed him in rehab and broke up the band. He pretty much obliterated their trust. And if he doesn't earn it back, I wouldn't be surprised if the tour bombs even harder than the album."

I keep my eyes on Ford, who is nodding like he knew I was going to say exactly what I did. But I don't look at West. I can't. As much as I'm disappointed in him for what he's done, I still don't want to hurt him. Because I've been on the other end of that hurt, and it sucks.

"And there's the real issue at hand," Ford says firmly. "Critic reviews have been just okay. The fan response hasn't been a fraction of what was expected.

The album is not proving out, on social media in particular, which, as you know, is everything these days. We couldn't figure out exactly why, much less come up with a solution until you provided one."

"Why didn't you tell me?" West's angry words are directed at Burke.

"Sorry, kid, I didn't know how. I knew what it would mean to you."

West's eyes flick between Jason and me. "Can we have a moment, please?"

Jason practically shoots out of his chair, and I realize just how superfluous he must have been feeling during this discussion. "Yes, of course. Max?" He tilts his head toward the door.

I nod and rise, leaving before I can give in to the urge to mouth to West, "I'm sorry." Because despite my own feelings toward him, I am. I never wanted to be the one to deliver such a harsh truth. Thanks to me, West has just been clued in to exactly how broken his life still is.

Hooker With a Penis by Tool

West

"So, anything else you've been hiding from me that I should know about?" It comes out with heaps of sarcastic anger, and I'm okay with that.

This is bullshit. How can the album possibly be doing so badly without me knowing? Except, I should've known. At the very least when Max tried to tell me. It annoys me almost more than I can stand that she was right.

Ford, the pretentious little fucker, glances nervously at Burke.

"We weren't trying to hide it, exactly," Burke grumbles. "You just had enough on your plate. But now you know. And now you also know why it's so important that we do this little apology project."

"Since when did the social media response to music become more important than what's actually good?" I muse out loud. Neither of them answers, not that I expected them to. "Whatever, man. I'm not happy about it, but I can't think of a better answer on the fly. Can't we regroup and go a different direction?"

I hate feeling trapped. And right now I feel like a baby bear in a cave that's just been woken by a hunter looking for a nice new throw rug. I'm not sure who's the hunter in this situation, Ford or Max. Regardless, Max may end up being the one to skin me alive publicly.

"Why not this?" Burke insists.

"Haven't we had this discussion?" I say with a sigh. "It's pandering, man. And so not rock and roll."

Ford fixes me with a disdainful look. "Worried about selling out?"

Now that makes me laugh. "Son, I sold out when you were about four years old. You can't not in this industry. But I'm also not about to do something that's contrary to the image we've worked hard to create."

"Even if that image isn't working for you anymore?" Ford asks pointedly.

I glare at him. I'm never so sullen as I am around

Ford. Dude's a dick, and it's all I can do not to punch him in his shiny face.

But unfortunately, the dick has a point. I guess that's his job, after all: maintaining our image. But I still don't get when and why social media became such a big deal. I bet it pisses Ford off too, come to think of it, not being able to completely control the message. Being subject to the ever-changing whims of the masses.

Welcome to my world, fucker. Once upon a time it was cool to be the troubled rock star. But when the consequences of living up to expectations go bad, they all turn on you in a flash, leaving you to pick up the pieces of your shattered life. I shake my head, pushing the bitter thoughts back into the shadows.

"So, what happens if I say I'm fine with things the way they are? That I don't want to play along with this game of Humiliate West?" I challenge.

"First," Ford replies arrogantly, "making you look human is not humiliating you. Only you can humiliate yourself if you continue to behave like a spoiled, entitled brat. Second, if you don't heed our recommendations, I'm afraid Nelson Public Relations will be unable to continue working in an advisory capacity to the band."

I fight back a snort at his pompous declaration, wondering if he passed that little change of strategy by his daddy before deciding on a course that could fuck over the family business.

"And I didn't want to have to play this card, but if you don't give the sponsors something to placate them ahead of the tour, your label is threatening to drop you too," Burke pipes up.

The label is ready to bolt? My head swings between them both. You've got to be fucking kidding me. Didn't I *just* ask if there was anything else they'd been keeping from me? I'm so pissed off I can practically feel the veins popping in my forehead.

But exploding will get me nowhere. I knew I was on thin ice. I guess I just didn't see the cracks had already started to form. And even I'm not stupid enough to keep pushing my limits.

"Fine. Get them back in here and let's get this over with."

With a smug grin, Ford rises and pops open the door just in time to hear Max's boss say, "We're not going to be the magazine that said no to Kristoffer Westberg. It would bury us."

"Sorry to interrupt," Ford says, not sounding sorry at all. "But we're ready for you." And with that he heads back to his seat, leaving the door open.

Max's boss comes back in, looking sheepish. Max follows looking downright pissed off. For some reason that pleases me.

"So, are we a go?" Jason asks, steepling his fingers under his chin.

"Absolutely," Ford insists. "The tour announcement is only six weeks away, so we need to get moving on this like yesterday."

"*Six weeks?*" Max blurts out. "That's insanity."

Jason gives her a sharp look.

"It's what we've got," Burke replies gruffly. "If that doesn't work for you we can go somewhere else —"

"No," Jason interrupts. "We'll make it work." He shoots another look at Max. "If Alexsis assists, that shouldn't be a problem, right, Max?" The tense undertone of "don't you dare fucking disagree with me in front of them" almost makes me laugh. I'm an asshole, but there it is.

Max takes a noticeable breath in through her nose, then responds tightly, "Of course. We'll make it work."

I fight a smile as I watch her, waiting for the obvious tension coiling her body to explode all over every damn one of us. And even with all the heavyweights in the room, I'm willing to bet Maxi Marshall's wrath is something to behold.

"Good," Ford all but purrs. "Now, Ms. Marshall. Since you were the one who came up with the idea, tell me: Who should West apologize to?"

Max gives him a bewildered look. "Aside from the fans, that's on West. How am I supposed to know everyone he's pissed off?"

"You know, that's a good point," Ford responds cryptically. "I think the fans may be the least of our agenda, actually. If we made this more personal, the fans would come just for the spectacle. And in a way, he'd be humbling himself to them *and* the people that they never even knew mattered to him."

Suddenly my humor at Max's discomfort evaporates and I shoot daggers toward Ford. Because I know exactly where he's going with this.

"We're not bringing my family into this," I interject tightly.

Ford turns toward me with a wolfish grin. "Is that who matters to you? Because if so, that's exactly what we need to do. I know humbling yourself isn't in your repertoire, West, but like it or not, that's exactly what you're going to do. And apologizing to your family, your friends, or whoever you actually *care* about … well, that's so much more impactful. Don't you think?"

I cross my arms over my chest and sink back into my chair, unwilling to rise to his bait. But that doesn't stop him.

"If you really care about the tour, the *fans*, I think that's exactly what needs to happen," he concludes, exuding smug-bastard vibes like it's going out of style.

Still, I keep my mouth shut, shaking my head slowly.

Burke's phone starts vibrating on the table. He silences it and looks up at me. "I have to get back to the office. You stay here and work with Ms. Marshall on the list. We'll get the contracts in place ASAP and start moving. Got that?"

He doesn't even wait for an answer, rising and shaking Jason's hand, doling out pleasantries before he leaves, dragging Ford with him.

"Well," Jason says awkwardly. "I guess I'll just leave you two to get on the same page."

Max looks pleadingly at Jason, but much to my amusement, he avoids her gaze and ducks out, closing the door behind him.

And she looks so perturbed, I can't help poking her just a little. "Well, Maxi. Here we are again. Alone at last."

Under Pressure by Queen & David Bowie

Max

The temptation to leave is strong. Anything not to have to look at West's stupid smirking face.

"Are you really going to make me do this?" I blurt out.

A wicked smile curls West's lips and he leans forward, getting dangerously close. "Seems like your boss is the one making you, based on the bit of hallway conversation we caught earlier."

"He's only making me because you asked. So un-ask," I push.

"Now, why would I do that? We have so much fun together, don't we, Maxi? Don't you wanna be my friend and help me out?" I don't answer, which makes him chuckle. "I'm a little disappointed, honestly. I'd counted on you getting us both out of this. But don't worry, if I have my way, neither of us will have to do this."

He's disappointed in *me*? Well, that's rich.

"Yeah, and exactly how do you plan to do that?" I snap.

"There's always another option, Maxi. Always."

My hackles rise, but I refrain from telling him to stop calling me "Maxi" because I'm pretty sure the more I do, the more he calls me that just to get a reaction.

"Another option? There isn't another option, West."

"Sure there is. Matter of fact I suggested one, but Burke wasn't having it."

"Well, it was probably some asinine self-serving suggestion like 'Party with West,'" I joke.

"It was 'Win a Date With West' actually," he corrects me.

There's no stopping the tide of uproarious laughter that bursts out of me. What. An. Arrogant. Bastard.

"It's not *that* funny," he grumbles, the butt-hurt-kid look back.

I wipe the tears of laughter from my eyes. "Oh, but it is. Really, though, I hate to be the only one to tell you the truth — again — but their solution is perfect. You're not going to convince them out of it."

"Perfect? How's that?"

I take a deep breath to calm the last remnants of laughter out of my system. So out of touch, this one. "Because this is going to be massively uncomfortable for you. And it's going to be a spectacle. People are going to gobble it up. Love you or hate you, *everyone* is going to want to watch a huge former rock star debase himself and, in all likelihood, get yelled at by a bunch of people who say all the things everyone's thinking. And then they get to watch you react to it. It's viral gold."

"*Former* rock star?" he asks acerbically.

I snort. "That's what you got from what I just said? Figures." I shake my head. "Look. You may as well just accept that this is going to happen." As soon as I say it, I realize that applies to me too. Fuck.

West smirks at me like he knows exactly what I'm thinking. And exactly how fucked I am by this too.

"Guess we're in for a ride, then."

"Yeah, well, we'll see about that," I grumble. Maybe I can convince Alexsis to step into a bigger role on this. Wouldn't be a hard sell, especially if it means more time with West.

"Oh, if I have to do this, you have to do this."

I purse my lips at him, considering that. "Are you at least going to apologize honestly?"

"I don't know, depends on who I have to apologize to."

"Right. So, the bare minimum."

"That about sums it up."

"This. This is why you've disappointed so many people," I say with exasperation.

"Now you sound like my old man, which isn't surprising, since I like him about as much as I like you." He pauses. "Okay, that might not be fair considering how much I loathe him."

I resist rolling my eyes at his declaration of dislike for me. I also resist saying it's very much mutual. Instead, I focus on what we have to do.

"Sounds like he might be a good place to start, then," I reply.

West's brows jump. "Oh no. Not gonna happen."

I raise an eyebrow in return. "You still think you can get out of this, don't you?" He doesn't respond, just smirks at me. The bastard. I rise, already so over arguing with him. "All right, I can see we aren't going to get anywhere with the list today. But you might want to start seriously considering stepping up for once in your life. Because if you don't … well, it's sure as hell going to hurt you more than it hurts me."

His face pulls together in confusion. Knowing I'm getting nowhere, I turn to leave.

"What if I told you going through this might be worse?"

I turn back and he's risen and is now standing just a couple of feet away.

"For you," I point out, returning one of his many smirks.

"I guess you're used to train wrecks," he replies, staring at me intently and radiating some seriously tormented vibes. "But I'm pretty over them at this point, Maxi. I want to get off this ride. I'm done being the bad guy."

My heart twinges in my chest at the reminder that he's just human. Not an untouchable rock star. He's a man. One who made some very bad choices and has suffered for them. Who doesn't realize or won't accept that he can't simply stop suffering for them whenever he chooses.

"Then start being the good guy," I reply.

The angst on his face is too much. I turn and walk out the door, leaving West alone with his demons.

7

Crucify by Tori Amos

West

"Stop, stop, stop!" Ward cries over the music, popping the mic back onto its stand. He whirls on me as the music dies off. "West, man, what the fuck?"

I jut my chin out, glaring at him. I know I'm fucking it up. But I also don't know how to not bite his head off right now.

He continues to stare at me expectantly. "Out with it. Your chords are harsh and out of tune. Which means you're in danger of snapping a string, or possibly even your beloved Rosie's beautiful little neck. If you need to burn off some anger, don't take it out on her, man."

I blow out a breath and slip the black leather strap over my head, gently seating Rosie on her stand.

I open my mouth. Then shake my head and close it. I prop my hands on my hips, digging deep to find a way to not be a whiny, aggressive little bitch.

"Reporter?" Michael asks from behind his set while twirling a drumstick.

I huff a laugh. "Not this time." I pause, my annoyance at Maxi Marshall simmering too close to the surface, even if she's not my biggest problem right now. But really, why does she have to be so irritating? I bet a good fuck would do her wonders … by someone other than me. Of course. I think. God, what's wrong with me? "Well, not exactly, anyway." I heave a sigh. Fine. Here goes. "I've been trying to come up with something to give the label and the sponsors that doesn't require heaping doses of public humiliation."

"Good luck with that," Nik says with a snort. "Ford told us what they want you to do. The public's going to lap that shit up, man. It'll be over in a few weeks. Just go with it."

My eyes meet hers, and I remember that she's the youngest of us all at twenty-six. And she's all over social media. If anyone in this room knows what they really want, it's her.

"Okay, fine. Maybe I get it, in theory. It's like a car wreck. You can't not look. But is that really going to translate to sales?" I ask. "I'm not convinced."

"Well, look at it this way," Michael says with a note of irritation in his voice. "If you *don't* do it, we're done. And some of us didn't have a huge rock career back in the day. For some of us this is our shot. You really gonna fuck that up for us?"

Nik shoots him a nervous glance. "Come on, man, give West a break. This is heavy shit. Would you wanna do it?"

"In a goddamn heartbeat," he replies without hesitation. "No apology tour, no shot. Even if it doesn't boost ticket sales, without it there are *no* ticket sales. It's a no-brainer." He's looking at and responding to Nik, but I'm hyperaware that every syllable is directed at me, and I can't help the rage it brings to the surface.

"That's easy to say when it's not you that's going to be served up as the media sacrifice of the summer in the name of entertaining the masses. I signed up to make music, not be a scapegoat for society's frustrations with famous people."

"How about just their frustrations with you, then?" James asks quietly. He looks up, his kind brown eyes meeting mine, and I can see the ache in them before he even continues. "Because that's the crux here, dude. It's time to stop being selfish. So you've got to decide, what's more important: your ego or the band?"

Pain lances through my heart. Is it really selfish not to want to be forced into this? Is this whole band against me? I look to Ward, who can barely meet my eyes.

He gives a half-hearted shrug. "I know it's difficult, but you have everything to lose if you don't do this, West. Stop wasting time trying to find a way out of it. There isn't. Their minds are made up. Own it and you have a shot at everything you want. Keep fighting it and, well, we're all going to lose."

I blink hard at the sting in my eyes, anger bubbling up from inside of me.

"I'd fight for you guys if you were in my shoes," I snap. "But sure. It's not like I haven't worked my ass off to get here. I'll just keep carrying everyone's burdens."

"Don't be such a fucking martyr," Michael snaps. "It's not like you didn't make this problem."

I clench my jaw so hard to keep from punching him in his stupid ginger face that I can hear my teeth straining under the pressure. The thought of cracking a tooth pisses me off even more. Wouldn't that just be the shit icing on this turd cake?

"Over the line," Ward barks at him. "If you're

lucky enough to get a taste of success you may understand someday how easy it is to fall into the sex-drugs-and-rock-and-roll trap."

"And what it costs you to climb back out," James agrees. "We're here for you, West. But it would seem you're not done climbing yet."

The threat of tears gets even more real, so I roughly grab Rosie and turn, done with this fucking conversation.

"Whatever. I'm out of here."

Because I can't stay. I can't break down here. I can't process this in front of these guys. Not even Ward.

I have a sudden need to self-medicate that is stronger than it has been since I started rehab. I need to get out of here. Now. I need to be alone so I can wrestle with the demons inside me.

THE OCEAN IS A PRETTY GOOD SUBSTITUTE FOR BOOZE, as it turns out. Its calming, endless undulation soothes the mind, body, and soul. Even though the sun has long since set over the horizon and the evening has cooled to the point that I have goose bumps, here I sit, on my balcony overlooking the Pacific Ocean, with

Rosie in my lap, absentmindedly strumming. Having made no real progress. Or anything even resembling a decision.

That's what they all want me to do. Decide. Only, there's really no decision to be made. Or is there?

The strumming turns into a melody and I hum along. Never quite singing. He beat that out of me a long time ago.

"You're going to make my ears bleed with that god-awful voice of yours!"

"What are you, killing a cat in there?"

"Shut up, kid, you couldn't carry a note in a bucket!"

I stop humming, heat creeping up my neck. Anger? Embarrassment? Who knows. But I keep strumming, the music a balm for every horrible thing he ever said or did to me to take my joy away. But there are some things that can't be taken from you, and love is one of them.

It's only been my love of music, of making something beautiful come out of the old, beat-up acoustic I'd inherited from a guy who was too embarrassed by it to take it to college with him, that pulled me through the abuse that was hurled at me.

He never criticized my playing, funnily enough, which is why I knew: I was good. I am good. But he had to direct his attentions somewhere, and Erik, my older brother, was a pro at making himself scarce. So it all landed on me. Better me than Annika, my younger sister. She had enough to carry. She was, after all, the one who killed mom. At least, according to my asshole father. Personally, I don't think dying in childbirth constitutes homicide, but then, I'm a good-for-nothing piece of shit — his words — so what do I know?

But twenty years and not enough miles later, he still can't take this from me.

It's that thought that breaks me. I'm taking this from myself if I can't swallow my pride. If I can't give them what they want by making it through a few stupid apologies.

My fingers scrape the strings, and I pull back when I feel the moisture. Shit. I'm crying all over my fucking guitar. I use my T-shirt to wipe Rosie off before lovingly setting her down next to me.

I furiously wipe the tears away, unwilling to surrender my composure to memories of the man who once broke me when I was just a boy. But now I'm the man, and if I do nothing else with my life, I need to be a better one than him.

"Then start being the good guy."

Maxi's words ring through my ears. As usual,

she's right. And she's wrong. Because it's just not that simple. It's not like I haven't tried to be. But apparently doing it my way hasn't been enough. So I guess it's time to do it their way.

8

The Hand That Feeds by Nine Inch Nails

Max

A few days later, I find myself back in the conference room discussing the apology tour project with Alexsis while we wait for West and the production company guy to show.

"So, like, what's your deal with West?" Alexsis asks, veering abruptly off the topic of who will research what.

"We don't have a deal," I reply defensively.

She tilts an eyebrow. "You *so* have a deal."

I shrug. "I was just a fan of the band for a long time, and then he broke them up. Kinda pissed me off and I don't pay attention to them anymore. End of story."

"Cute. But I meant now, not then."

"I don't know what you're talking about."

"I'm talking about the sexual tension I could practically smell across the office both times he was here."

I wrinkle my nose in disgust. "Then sexual tension must smell a lot like hostility because there's a lot of that going in both directions," I reply firmly.

"Oh please," Alexsis scoffs. "It's schoolyard basics. Boys only tease you when they like you."

I look her straight in the eye. "That's bullshit. Boys tease you to get a reaction out of you so they can fulfill their own need to feel in control. West is angry because I'm a female who doesn't want to jump his bones. So he teases me to feel like he has some control over me. Same reason he wants me to do this whole 'apology tour' crap."

"Well, that's an interesting theory," comes a voice from the door.

I look up to find West smirking at us.

For a moment, I'm tempted to be embarrassed. But you know what? Fuck that.

"Ah. There you are. Perfect timing," I say sweetly, with the most saccharine smile I can muster.

"Perfect to join in the West bashing? Because

that's the party I'm here for," he says, sauntering in and plopping down at the head of the table.

I'm taken aback by his response, but before I can reply, Jason, Ford, and a third man with sandy hair and round glasses enter the room.

"All right," Ford begins, taking a seat next to Alexsis. "West. What's our lineup?"

Jason sits next to me, while the stranger settles at the end of the table.

"Oh, this is Carter Lonnergan, head of the production team for this project," Ford adds as an afterthought. "Carter, this is Max Marshall and …" Ford turns, realizing for the first time that Alexsis is next to him. And clearly he likes what he sees. He's checking her out so hard that Alexsis blushes as we all watch.

"This is Alexsis Monaghan," I offer.

"Alexsis," Ford says. "So nice to meet you."

Alexsis smiles demurely, and I can't tell if she's into him or not.

"So, the lineup?" West prompts Ford.

"Yes, of course. The lineup. What have you got?" Ford responds.

West leans back in his chair, his gaze shifting to Carter. "How many stops do I get?"

Carter shrugs. "Depends on where they are."

"Mostly around L.A.," he responds. "One in San Francisco."

"That's not much travel, so probably as many as you've got," Carter replies. "We've got a few weeks to shoot, then we'll need a few weeks in post."

West nods. "Okay, here's what I'm thinking." He leans forward and raises a fist, putting up a thumb. "The band. I don't know if you want that as a group or individually."

"Hmmm. Let me think about that. Keep going," Carter says.

West throws up a finger. "My older brother. He's out in Corona."

"Why your older brother?" Ford asks, finally fully engaged.

West shoots him a wary look. "We haven't spoken in fifteen years. He was the first to walk away when he found out I was using."

Ford nods his approval, so West throws up another finger and sighs. "Sadie Sullivan. The groupie who introduced me to cocaine. We were together when the band went down."

Carter lets out a low whistle. "Well, that ought to make for good TV."

West ignores him, throwing up another finger. "My little sister. She's in San Francisco," he says to Carter.

"And why her?"

West inhales slowly, clearly reluctant to answer. "I introduced her to a guy. She followed him there. It wasn't a good thing."

My throat tightens as I read between the lines, but I make a mental note to ask him about it privately. Nobody else says a word, so West continues, throwing up the last finger on that hand.

"My dad." The last word comes out broken and hoarse. West clears his throat. "Also in Corona."

"We could do the dad and the brother at the same time," Carter offers in Ford's direction.

West shakes his head. "You can't. Take my word for it."

Carter's eyes widen a fraction. "All right. That all?"

"The fans. But …"

"What?" I prompt, my curiosity forming the word before I can stop myself.

"I think we should do something more than a meet and greet."

"What are you thinking?" Ford ask, clearly also curious.

"I'm thinking a small private concert," West explains quietly. "We let the fans know what it's for and have them submit something on why they should be chosen. One of you can decide how that all goes down. But at least it would help us find the ones who need that reconciliation the most."

The room is dead silent when he's finished. Finally, Ford speaks up.

"I'm impressed. That's a fantastic idea, West."

I would never say it out loud, but I actually agree. And for the first time, I feel like maybe this whole thing has a chance.

"Thanks," West replies, lifting a finger and beginning to trace circles into the tabletop.

"That's all a great jumping off point," Ford continues. "Our team has also discussed and agreed that there needs to be strong social media involvement throughout. TikToks of before each apology appeal. Reaction Instagram Reels of after — without spoilers, of course. Both are to give tidbits without giving too much away. We're also planning an airing party where the official tour is announced. It'll be aired on IGTV, Facebook, and YouTube." He pauses, tapping his fingers on the table. "Given your idea, I think maybe we should hold the private concert after the apologies so we can include it in the airing. Though we could also livestream the event itself on Facebook for full exposure and impact."

"That sounds like a lot," West says apprehensively.

"And that doesn't include the magazine," I pipe

up. West gives me a look that's almost desperate. "But I'll have Alexsis push all that material we'll already be doing to our website. I may just need additional time around each visit to ask questions that are for the article."

"Great. It's settled then. West, Max, and Alexsis will work on preparing for the apologies and social media posts. I'll contact Burke to arrange the private concert. Carter and I will contact your family and the band to schedule shoots."

"I'm sorry, you'll what now?" West asks sharply.

"Would you rather blindside them?" Ford returns just as cuttingly.

The two men stare at each other so fiercely I swear the temperature in the room rises.

"No. I guess not," West finally agrees. "But I'm not sure they'll all agree."

Ford's mouth lifts on one side. "Oh, I think they'll all want to hear you grovel. But if they don't, I'm prepared to persuade them."

I'm immediately disgusted by his implication, but West beats me to speaking.

"You are *not* paying anyone off to do this, Nelson," he says angrily.

Ford smiles. "I'll do what it takes to save your career." He pauses, tilting his head. "Won't you?"

I've never seen someone look as much like a

trapped animal as West does at that question. I'm pretty sure if West had claws, Ford would be lying on the floor right now trying to keep his insides from falling out.

"Of course," West replies in the least convincing tone I've ever heard.

"Good." Ford makes to leave, patting West condescendingly on the shoulder as he passes. "Play nice now, kids. Carter?"

"Yes, sir." Carter leaps up and follows, leaving the rest of us in the room.

"Kids?" Jason scoffs. "What is that guy, like twelve?"

"He's twenty-four. So yeah, pretty much twelve," West replies.

Jason shakes his head, rising. "Well, once again, I think I've proved I'm pretty much useless here. I'll be in my office if you need me," he says to me.

I smile up at him gratefully. But once he's gone, and it's just me, Alexsis, and West …

"Alexsis, can you give West and I some time alone?" I ask quietly.

"Of course," Alexsis replies, jumping up and darting out of the room before I can even blink. Okay. Maybe she is interested in Ford. Because I get the feeling she only agreed so quickly so she could try to catch him before he leaves.

As soon as she's gone, I shake my head. "I sure hope Ford and Alexsis don't start something or Alexsis is going to be useless to me."

West fixes me with a smirk. "Seems like you may think she's already useless to you. Because I know you really don't want to be alone with me."

"Now, that's where you're wrong," I say. "I thought it might be easier to do what's next with just us."

"Mhm, you keep telling yourself that," he murmurs. "But I know you're starting to come around."

I roll my eyes. "You wish."

West leans forward, rubbing his bottom lip with his thumb as if in thought. "I'm starting to wonder if maybe I do," he replies.

Something inside my chest catches, and I clamber to keep the conversation moving forward. "So. The apologies. We're starting with the band?" I prompt, hoping my desperate attempt to turn the attention away from what he said isn't obvious. Then again, I don't care if it is, as long as we move on.

West's dark eyes search mine for a moment. And for that moment all I can do is hope he doesn't keep teasing me. Or I may really start coming around. He does seem to suddenly be awfully cooperative, and some of his ideas were really thoughtful.

"Yes." He says, then he blinks and leans back. "The band. Well, mostly Ward and James. But Nik and Michael have put up with an awful lot of my shit for the last year and a half too."

"Hmmm. But surely you'll have more to say to Ward and James?"

West lifts a shoulder. "James is too laid back to care about apologies, really. I think he forgave me *while* I was fucking everything up. But Ward? He's different. He acts like he doesn't care, so I acted like I didn't either."

"But he does."

West nods slowly. "I think of anyone, I owe him an apology the most."

"Maybe we should save him until last then?"

West huffs a laugh. "I may owe him the most, but he will be the absolute least drama."

"Ah," I say, realizing what he's done. "You ordered them in what you think will be the least to the most difficult."

He dips his head in confirmation. "Yes, ma'am."

"Now I'm 'ma'am'?" I ask dryly. "I think I prefer Maxi." I almost face-palm as soon as the words are out of my mouth. He shoots me a mischievous grin, and I suspect I'm going to be ma'amed constantly for the next six weeks. Christ.

"Moving on," I continue swiftly. "The older brother. Not going to be much drama?"

"I'd bet no. He's a runner, not a fighter. He spent most of our childhood out of the house just to avoid, well, everything. Anyway, I think he might have some harsh things to say, but that's about it."

"Do you think he'll forgive you?" I ask curiously.

West spreads his arms. "I'm clean and sober. He never had an issue with the rock star bit. Just the drugs."

"Who had a problem with the rock star bit?"

West's face falls. "Don't worry, we'll get there."

I squint at him for a minute, debating whether I want to press the issue. But I guess if we'll get there…

"The ex?" I prompt.

West grins. "That is going to be big drama. Sadie never disappoints."

"So again, why not put her last?"

"I may be dreading that one, but I'd rather face her before I face my dad."

"And your sister?"

"You're a little too good at your job, you know that?" he asks, scratching the back of his head.

"Am I making you uncomfortable?" I tease. Kind of hoping I am. It's a small payback for all his bull-shit, but I'll take it.

"I don't know. Why don't you try asking what you really want to know?" he pushes back.

Well, shit. He's more perceptive than I gave him credit for. But fine. He wants it direct? That's certainly something I'm good at.

"You introduced your sister to drugs, didn't you?"

"Damn, Maxi, you don't fuck around," he teases, though the heavy sigh following belies his distress. "Yes. I did. And to my drug *dealer* while I was at it; he's the fucker she left with."

I nod lightly, studying him. He looks tired.

"Why are you suddenly being so cooperative?" I ask curiously.

He cocks an eyebrow. "I'm not stupid enough to bite the hand that feeds me," he replies carefully.

"I see." Though I feel like there's more to this. But I'm sure I'll have plenty of time with him over the coming weeks to figure it out. "And your dad?"

"That's going to take more time to explain that you've got right now."

I lean back in my chair and cross my legs like I'm just getting settled in. "I've got all the time in the world."

"Yeah, well, I don't. I've got places to be, Maxi. How about we talk about that another day? Since he's last and all, there should be plenty of time. Wouldn't want you to get sick of me too quick." He winks, but I see no cuteness in his eyes. He's just done.

"Fine. This is your shit show," I concede, rising to show him out.

"You don't know the half of it," he mutters as he follows.

His tone makes me wonder if I really want to know the other half. But like it or not, I'm pretty sure all of West's dirty secrets are going to be bared for everyone to see, with me in the front row seat. While I can't feel too sorry for him, seeing as he mostly brought it on himself, I also can't say I envy him. Because the shit show has only just begun.

9

All Apologies by Nirvana

West

"So, we're gonna like, just start? I don't get a list of questions ahead of time or something?" I ask, shifting nervously on the rehearsal room couch.

Maxi rolls her eyes. Cute.

"That wouldn't be very spontaneous," she points out, twisting around to shuffle in her bag.

"Yeah, that's kinda the idea," I mumble.

"What was that?" she asks, whipping back around.

"Nothing." I smirk and shove my hands in my pockets. We haven't even started apology number one and I'm already over it.

Carter and one of his minions walk in hauling yet

another load of camera and lighting equipment. They go back to adjusting the setup pointed at the couch.

"Do I at least get to know who's up first?" I poke.

Maxi finally emerges from her giant bag holding a moleskin notebook and pen.

"You are," she says with a sly smile.

I narrow my eyes at her briefly but remember my resolution to play along. Well, as much as I'm capable of. I have my own internal bet on when I'm going to hit my limit, but that's neither here nor there right now. Maxi wants to play just us? I'm definitely down with that.

"All right," I agree. "What do you want to know?"

Maxi looks back at Carter. "We ready?" He gives her the thumbs up, the makeup chick darts in to powder our faces for the seventeenth time, and then the countdown begins.

And then we're rolling.

Goddamn, I forgot how it feels to be in front of a camera. It's like the first time you stick your hand down a girl's panties. You feel like you have no idea what you're doing, but you're excited. And one wrong move and your night is toast.

"So, West, with this interview, you've officially begun your apology tour. How are you feeling right now?"

I wasn't expecting her to dive in like that, and I

gotta admit it throws me a little. It begins indeed. I do not, thankfully, spit out what was just going through my head. At least I have that much presence of mind.

"Gotta say, Maxi, I'm nervous," I reply with a grin that's contrary to the truth I spoke. But the way her mouth tightens when I call her Maxi makes me smile wider. Maybe this will be fun after all.

"I don't blame you. You're about to apologize to your bandmates, new and original." She pauses, presumably for effect. "Who are you *most* nervous to apologize to today?"

I take a deep breath and puff it out. Also for effect.

"I think you all probably know," I reply, donning a humble look for the camera. "While all my bandmates deserve an apology, no one deserves one more than Ward."

"You and Ward Pierce have been friends for a long time. But then, the same could be said of James Kennedy, couldn't it?"

I dip my head in agreement. "Yes. We're all like brothers. But James was smart enough to stay away from the temptations that came with the gig. Ward was always right there next to me, yet somehow stayed on the right side of the line." I chuckle dryly. "Well, the less worse side of the line."

"Not your side of the line, you mean?" Maxi asks, looking from me to the camera.

The question makes me feel more defensive than I know I have any right to.

"The non-addict side of the line."

Maxi has no cute retort for that. They never do when you drop the A-bomb.

"Anyway," I continue as if it's no big deal — even though it's a very big fucking deal — "because he was closer to it all, he suffered more of the consequences of my behavior than James did." Not that they didn't both suffer. We all did.

"Ah, like the time you both got arrested after the Vegas concert in 2017?"

Just the mention of that night has my eyes dropping in embarrassment. And the booze-deprived monster deep within wakes up. I'm not sure if it's the mention of that epically embarrassing night, or because of the nerves that expand beyond my ability to rein them in. My finger finds my knee, drawing soothing circles. Calming it back to sleep.

"Yes, like that," I agree, looking back up and holding Maxi's curious gaze.

She swallows hard, and I know she gets how low of a blow that question was. But then, that's what this whole charade is about, right? A bunch of low blows I'm expected to take because I had a problem I couldn't handle on my own, borne of equal parts my own bullshit and the temptations I couldn't avoid.

"I see. It sounds like he's definitely the most deserving of an apology." She pauses. "I guess we'd better get started then," she replies blithely.

As if on cue — wait, of course it was a cue — Ward walks through the door and around Maxi to sit next to me on the couch. Exactly how we've sat so many times recently, Ward as ever acting as my moral compass, reality check, and shoulder to whine on all in one. Because I don't cry on anyone's shoulder, least of all Ward's. In front of the TV, watching *Moana*? Like a little girl. But never in front of Ward.

And yet, for some reason, as he sits down, smiling in that reassuring way he does, I feel tears prick the back of my eyes. Fuck.

Happy thoughts. Rosie. Guitar Center. Tits.

There, that did it. Tears gone.

"Hey, man," he greets me with a grin.

I reach out and we fist bump. "'Sup, dude."

We both laugh and I look back at Maxi, who begins asking Ward a bunch of dumbass questions about when we met, moments that "defined our friendship," and a bunch of other touchy-feely bullshit. None of his answers are unexpected, but then before I'm ready, Maxi turns to me.

"So, you guys have been through thick and thin, and here you are now," she sums up. "West, do you have anything you'd like to say to Ward?" She cocks an eyebrow, clearly signaling me to do my thing.

Well, all right then. I take a deep breath and turn to Ward.

"You don't have to say it," Ward offers, his smile slipping to the side.

"Oh, I'm gonna say the shit out of," I assure him. I look back at Maxi again. "Can I say shit on TV?" I look at the camera. "Probably not. I probably shouldn't say fuck either then, right?"

Maxi face-palms. "We'll edit it later," she mumbles.

"Just keep going," Carter says from behind the camera.

I turn back to Ward and my smile hitches. "I'm sorry, Ward." The words feel better than I thought. And suddenly they start pouring out. "I'm sorry I've never said I'm sorry. I'm sorry for all the times you had to follow my drunk, stoned ass around trying to keep me from epically fucking up." I glance up at the camera. Pretty sure that was two things I shouldn't say on TV. Oops. I give a mildly apologetic look before turning back. "But most of all I'm sorry it wasn't enough. That I wasn't strong enough to —"

"You had me at 'sup dude," he says jokingly. But I know what he means. I'm already forgiven.

There are those damn tears again. I blink hard and

nobody is more shocked than me when I practically tackle Ward in a hug. A bro hug, of course. I pat him on the back and pull away as soon as I realize what I'm doing.

I look over at Maxi, and she's looking at me like I just kicked her puppy.

"Carter, can we pause or cut or whatever?" she asks.

Carter, now seated to the left of the camera, looks up from behind his computer and nods.

Maxi turns back, her eyes narrowed sharply. "That was too easy."

I cock an eyebrow. "I'm … sorry?" I reply. I didn't even mean to mock her. It's just a gift.

She rolls her eyes. "Come on, West. If we're going to do this, you actually have to do it. None of this over-the-top fake apologizing stuff." She turns to Ward. "Did you guys practice this, or do you just naturally BS for the camera?"

Ward stares back impassively. "Define 'practice,'" he replies slowly.

Maxi throws her hands up and makes a disgusted noise. It's too fucking funny watching her lose her shit, but I also don't want to be here all damn day.

"Keep your panties on, we didn't practice. That was all classic West and Ward," I assure her.

"Really? Because it sounded extremely rehearsed.

On your end at least." Her eyes flick back to Ward. "And 'you had me at 'sup dude'? Really?"

Ward finally cracks a grin. "I thought it was funny."

I thought it was funny too, but I don't say that out loud. Instead I hold up a fist and he bumps his against mine.

"So not taking things seriously is going to be a theme here," Maxi grumbles. "All right then. I take it back. If this is authentic, then I guess that's what we've got to work with."

"As authentic as J. Lo's booty," I assure her.

"Or Tyra Banks' tits," Ward offers.

"Can we stop talking about famous women's body parts, please?" Maxi begs, clearly sorry she ever stopped to question us.

I don't even try to contain the smirk because I know how much it gets under her skin. And sure enough, her eyes angrily dart to my mouth.

"Are we ready then?" Carter asks dryly, causing all of our heads to turn toward him.

He's so quiet I'd kinda forgotten he was there.

"Let's do this. Rest of the band, then?" I prompt.

Carter nods and whirls a finger high in the air.

One of his assistants counts us down and we're back to business.

"And just like that, all's forgiven," Maxi says

sweetly, tipping her head to the side. Then her eyes go comically wide. "Oh, but what about the rest of the band?"

Another cue, clearly, as James, Nik, and Michael file in.

A couple of assistants pop into the room, adding chairs for Nik and Michael as James sits on my other side on the couch.

The process repeats on a much lower-key level, with each member of the band talking about our history, me offering a token apology, and them accepting.

Then Carter has each individual band member sit on the couch alone and talk to Maxi about how they feel about me, where the band's at, and our future. Again, nothing surprising. Or rather, the only surprise is how nobody seems to have anything really bad to say about me. Disappointments here and there, sure, but nothing as bad as stuff I've thought about myself in my own head. Or about what they must have thought at some point. So, either they're playing nice for the cameras or they really are just that awesome.

As cynical as I can be sometimes, I kind of hope it's the latter.

In any case, this was meant to be the easy one. Because it's only going to get harder from here.

Finally, what feels like hours later, they have us

"rehearse" while they take some filler footage, and then we're done.

As I'm packing away Rosie, Maxi approaches me.

"What are you still doing here?" I ask, zipping up the gig bag.

"They wanted me for some additional post footage," she grumbles.

"Aww, so you didn't get to hear us rehearse? Bet you're really sorry you missed that," I tease.

"Oh I caught the end of it," she assures me. "It's not like I haven't heard you play before."

"Ah, but up close and personal is different."

"I've heard you play up close and personal," she retorts, hands flying to her hips.

"Oh *really?* When was that?" I ask, actually curious.

"A long time ago," she says, her expression abruptly closing down. "Anyway. Carter asked me to remind you to *not* prepare for talking to your brother. They want it as —"

"Spontaneous as possible, I know, Christ," I swear. "Any idea when that little party's going to happen, or do I just get called in morning-of like today?"

Maxi shrugs. "Next week sometime. We'll all have to get there at the same time, so I imagine there will be a bit of a heads up."

I suppress a sigh, unwilling to show any emotion

around this woman. She'd probably eat me alive at the first sign of weakness. Normally I'm fine flying by the seat of my pants. But this … this is like waiting for a bunch of surprise ass-whoopings. As if I didn't already have enough anxiety on a daily basis.

Maxi watches me curiously as I process.

"Stop shrinking me right now," I tell her.

She blushes bright red. "You just looked, I dunno, upset. I wasn't 'shrinking' you. But …"

"What?" I press.

One of her shoulders lifts. "As much as this is the last thing I want to be doing, I know it's probably the same for you. Harder, even. I know you're getting the worse end of the deal here, so I'm trying make this go as smoothly as possible, and that includes making sure you're okay."

I scoff. "Even though you hate me?"

She returns my scoff with interest. "I don't *hate* you. That would require feeling something for you. And that's not a road I ever plan to travel down again."

Oh, well, now she's got my attention. "You saying you used to feel something for me, Maxi?" I ask with a sly grin, leaning toward her. Joke's on me, though, because she smells like lilacs and rain. Damn.

She stiffens at my proximity. "I was young and stupid. You can't possibly hold that against me."

I immediately think to myself, *I've got plenty of things I'd like to hold against you.* And then I internally bitch-slap myself. What the hell, West?

"I don't," I reply abruptly. "And you don't need to feel for me. I'm fine." And with that, I haul Rosie off the table and get the fuck out of there. Away from everything that conversation stirred. Revulsion at being pitied. Attraction toward someone who has made my life into this hell. My own anxieties.

I spend the whole drive home thinking about all those things and more. But as I fall asleep that night, it's just Maxi on my mind, and I want to kick my own ass.

I don't get off on chasing girls who don't want to "feel something for me." I like my women willing and into it.

So why can't I stop thinking about Maxi Marshall?

10

Swallow My Pride by The Ramones

Max

Almost a full week goes by before the next stop on the tour. I stand in the parking lot of the location just north of Corona, hands on hips, while Carter and his crew scramble around between two vans and the building, getting everything set up.

"So, what genius picked a bowling alley?" I ask Alexsis with more than a hint of sarcasm in my tone.

She laughs. "That would be Erik Westberg, West's older brother."

I look at her in surprise. "Really? Because this seems like something Ford would insist on. You know, to make West look like just a normal kind of guy."

Alexsis purses her lips. "You said that like you think Ford is —"

"A little full of himself? Yes, yes I do think that."

"He's actually a really nice guy," she returns with a frown.

"Oh *really*?" I ask with interest. "And how do we know this?" Though I'm pretty sure I know.

She grins, twirling a lock of blond hair around a finger. "Because he may have taken me to dinner last weekend."

I slap her playfully on the shoulder. "And you didn't tell me this until now?" I gasp accusingly. "For shame, Alexsis, for shame."

"I didn't know if it was okay, but I couldn't hold it in any longer," she admits.

I smile, remembering the elated feeling that comes with the start of something new. Not that I've felt it in a long time. But it's hard to contain, equal parts hope and delicious tension.

But before I can ask for more details, a car with tinted windows rolls up. "Yeah, well, you may want to hold on to the rest until later. Looks like Ford's least biggest fan just arrived."

And proving my point, West climbs out of the back. His hair looks damp and instead of his usual plain-black tee, he's wearing a Ramones T-shirt. Black, of course, with the band name and logo on it.

"The entertainment has arrived," he says grandly, stretching his arms out. Then he looks up and frowns. He catches my eye and points at the building. "Maxi, what the fuck are we doing at a bowling alley?"

I can't help it, his confused, indignant tone makes me burst out laughing.

"Hope you brought your bowling shoes," I tease, pulling Alexsis toward the building.

West trails behind us, his long legs quickly eating up the ground between us. "No, seriously, are we really doing this here?" he asks.

"Apparently," I confirm.

And to my surprise, West laughs. "Erik."

It wasn't a question, so I just look at him, waiting for an explanation. But he doesn't provide one, following us into the building.

As we approach the desk, I can see Carter and crew setting up at one of the lanes. Oh boy. We're really doing this.

"I hope nobody expects me to bowl," Alexsis pipes up.

I huff a laugh. "Don't worry, I think West gets that honor."

West smirks at us both. "Yes, well, let's get this show on the road then, shall we?"

"Your brother's not here yet," I return. "At least, not as far as I know."

"Perfect," West says, rubbing his hands together. "That'll give me time to warm up. Do we have the place to ourselves?"

I give him a bewildered look. Does he really bowl? He cocks an eyebrow, waiting for an answer.

"Um. Yes. I think we do," I respond, still completely baffled by this turn of events.

"Excellent," he hums, turning toward the desk and engaging the attendant to get his shoes.

"Alexsis," I mumble.

"Yeah?"

"Are we really about to watch Kristoffer Westberg bowl?"

"Weird, right?" she replies. I glance over at her, and she's looking at West with the exact expression I feel right now. It's just too unreal.

"I have to admit," I say slowly. "I've interviewed a lot of musicians. But I've never done an interview while they're bowling. I have no clue how we're going to pull this off."

She shrugs. "I say we go with it. What's the worst that could happen?"

Famous last words.

Who knew West could bowl? Who knew West even liked bowling? Not this former superfan, that's for damn sure. And yet, as we finished setting up, that's exactly what he did, and he did it pretty damn well, all while answering questions about his brother.

He was, once again, more forthcoming than I'd expected, explaining how his brother had always been about doing the "right thing" — aka what their dad wanted — all while somehow avoiding the man himself as much as possible.

He did skirt around the issues with his dad again, but openly talked about how much he hated his brother as a kid and that now, as an adult, he can see more where he was coming from.

It's the first time Kristoffer Westberg has surprised me in a good way in a very long time, and it gives me hope that this will be another successful apology. Ford and Burke seemed happy with the first one, anyway, so I figured if this went the same way, then we'd be in good shape.

Luckily, once his brother did show, things seemed to take off on their own between the two of them and they didn't even need me. Like, at all. West and his brother had a very natural conversation about West's time in rehab and how he's been clean more than two years now.

His brother not only forgave without being asked

but also asked for West's forgiveness for the disappearing acts he apparently used to pull on the regular. It was almost touching. There wasn't any hugging like with West and Ward, rather a friendly handshake.

And now, Alexsis is interviewing Erik in another part of the building while I get ready to do West's post interview.

As I sit down to West taking off his bowling shoes, he looks up at me and my heart trips in my chest. He looks *happy*. If I hadn't gotten to know him better, I wouldn't be able to tell. But his smirk is more a smile, and there's a light in his eyes I don't often see. It takes me a moment to place what it makes me feel: pleased. I'm pleased that he's happy.

I sink into the closest orange plastic chair, unsure why that weirds me out so much.

"You know, I know you're here to do my post-apology interview thing. But I realized there's something very important we haven't addressed," he says.

"Oh? What's that?"

"We haven't talked about your taste in music. I think I need to find out what kind of rock expert you really are before I answer any more questions," he says, leaning back in his chair.

"And how, exactly, do you plan to do that?" I ask suspiciously.

"Just a few harmless questions of my own." But

the mischievous glint in his eye betrays him. He's feeling peppy and looking to test me. But two can play at that game.

"Hm. How about this. You get to ask me one, then I get to ask you one?"

He cocks an eyebrow. "Fine," he agrees.

"All right, you go first," I tell him.

His answering grin is feline. "Fender or Gibson?"

I level a look at him. He knows that I know how much he loves his precious Gibson guitar. His pride and joy. His *Rosie*. "Fender."

He laughs. "I knew you were going to say that."

"Mhm," I murmur. "Jimmy Page or Eric Clapton?"

"Jimmy Page," he returns with no hesitation. Good man. "Rolling Stones or The Beatles?"

I scoff. "The day we met I was wearing a Stones shirt, dude."

"Still a valid and very fundamental question," he defends.

I roll my eyes. "Rolling Stones, obviously. Bohemian Rhapsody or Stairway to Heaven?"

He's actually quiet for a minute. "Bohemian Rhapsody."

That surprises me, given how iconic Stairway to Heaven is, especially with guitarists.

"Don't tell anyone I said that, though," he follows up.

"Your secret's safe with me," I promise.

"All right, all right. Now. A very important question." He turns his head and gives me a serious look. "Who would win in a fight between Billy Corgan and Courtney Love?"

I bark a sharp laugh. "Courtney Love, hands down. For reasons I assume are obvious."

He chuckles and nods.

"Bon Scott or Brian Johnson?" I ask.

"Damn, you're not pulling punches, are you, Maxi?" he says with a teasing tone. "Bon Scott."

"Really? It's not just because he's the original, is it?"

West shrugs. "Sometimes you can't forget the one who made you fall in love." His eyes meet mine.

I swallow hard. He just said a mouthful. "So did I pass?"

He narrows his eyes at me. "Yeah, I guess you're okay."

My eyebrows jump of their own accord. Well, that's a shift. Here I was thinking I was the biggest, or at least most recent, thorn in his side. Now I'm *okay*. Interesting. Guess we'll see how long *that* lasts.

"Glad we got that out of the way," I reply. "So can I do my job now?"

He slings an arm over the chairs, staring at me with a glint in his eyes. "Yeah, Maxi. Go for it."

I fight the urge to roll my eyes because I get it. He wants to feel like something about this is on his terms. Under his control. All things considered, his test was actually pretty enjoyable.

Oh god, did I really just think of West and "enjoyable" in the same sentence? I must be getting soft.

As soon as Carter's assistant is ready and we're rolling again, I purposely don't go easy on West, grilling him on his conversation with his brother. I even get him to squirm at one point. I'm a bit sadistically happier about that than I should be.

But whatever little measure of control he took, I needed back. Because when it comes to West, I can't trust myself; there's too much of my past that was spent adoring him, and I've had to shake myself out of those patterns. So I need to stay in the driver's seat here.

We finally get everything we need, and Alexsis and I compare notes before we pack up and head home for the evening.

I check in with Carter before leaving, and he gives me the news: The next apology is this Sunday. West's ex. I don't know whether to dread whatever drama is bound to unfold or plan on bringing popcorn.

As I head out to my car, ruminating over that, I

don't even see West leaning against exterior of the building just outside the entrance.

"Hey, Maxi."

I look up, startled. "What are you still doing here?"

"I'm waiting for my driver."

"Can't you call an Uber or something? Or is that not safe for formerly famous rock stars?"

"Ouch, Maxi, ouch," he sighs. "I prefer my guy. At least, for another year anyway, until I can get my license back."

I shrug, finding it hard to feel sorry for someone who had multiple DUIs within a couple of years. "Did you need something?"

"I heard Carter talking about Sadie."

"Sadie? Oh, your ex?"

"That's the one. Sunday?"

"Sunday," I confirm. "You ready?"

He shakes his head and laughs. "Never."

A drop hits my nose, causing me to look up. "Oh shit, it's —"

"Raining," West finishes as the small drops promptly turn into a deluge. Well, for Southern California anyway. "Fuck."

"Come on," I call, running toward my car. "Get in."

He doesn't hesitate, running the short distance and

practically diving into the passenger seat as I get in the driver's side of my tiny coupe.

A glance in the rearview mirror tells me I look like a drowned rat, though thankfully my makeup isn't visibly running. But I look over at him, and his T-shirt is soaked through, sticking to the lean muscles of his chest. Drops of water run over his sharp cheekbones. In short, he looks like a wet fucking dream. The bastard.

"Where's your driver?" I ask.

"Downtown. I can wait for him inside."

I shake my head, resigned. "In this weather? It'll take him hours to get here. I'm in Culver City, I'll drop you off on my way home."

"I don't *live* downtown, that's just where he is. But I can get a ride from Culver City."

"So where do you *live*?" I poke back.

"The Palisades."

I snort. "Figures." Shaking my head, I buckle in and start the car. Why on earth did I just sign up for an hour or two stuck in a car with this guy?

Because I'm not an asshole, that's why. If I were, this would be so much easier. Well, this wouldn't *be* at all, as I'd have refused to see him the first time he showed up at *Rock Scene*. But that's not who I am, so here we are. Dripping wet and fogging up the windows of my car while I drive the former rock god who shaped my younger years across Los Angeles. Life is weird.

"Thank you," West says, breaking through my thoughts as I pull onto the main road.

I glance over at him. Still looking like he just won a wet T-shirt contest. If they even have those for dudes.

"You're welcome," I reply begrudgingly.

He beams. "That was really hard for you to say, wasn't it?"

An unbidden laugh chokes its way out of me. "Yes!"

"What'd I do, Maxi? To make you not want to feel anything for me anymore?"

"Why do you care?" I deflect. "You don't like me either."

"That's what I thought too. But I'm starting to think I may have been a bit hasty on that front."

I shoot him a skeptical look.

"No, really. You didn't have to drive me home. You didn't have to do *any* of this, really. But you are. You're obviously a good person, Maxi. So if there's a problem here, it must be me."

His words hit me right in the heart. "You're not a bad person, West."

"Thanks," he murmurs. But from his tone I can tell he doesn't agree.

I glance over to see him rubbing circles into his knee with one finger.

"Why do you do that?" I ask, nodding toward his hand.

"You ask a lot of questions but won't answer any?"

I laugh. "That's literally my job description," I remind him.

"Fair enough," he allows. "Off the record?"

I debate that. But if we're going to be in this for another, what, three or four apologies? Anyway, we're going to need to build some sort of trust here.

"Off the record," I agree.

"It's a soothing mechanism." He pauses. "For when I feel like drinking."

I look over at him in shock. Because he does it *so* much.

"Yeah. I feel like drinking a lot," he says, as if replying to my thoughts.

"Wow. I had no idea you still struggled so much."

He shrugs. "It's not as bad as it was at first."

"But at least you're not an addict anymore," I offer. "You've got your life back. You'll get there."

A small smile graces his still-damp lips, and he looks at me with those dark, soulful eyes of his. "I'll always be an addict, Maxi. But I'm still me. Always have been, always will be. Even addiction can't take that away. Nothing can, really."

I swallow hard against the emotions his words stir in me. Pity. Compassion. Confusion.

"Why are you telling me this?" I ask, my throat dry as I try my hardest to concentrate on driving. But now that we're on the freeway, slowed to a crawl, it doesn't require enough of my focus to ignore the gnawing feeling in my stomach. *Guilt.* Even though I know that particular emotion should be all him.

"So you know I'm still that guy you felt for once. In here." He thumps his fist to his heart.

I blink hard against the tears. Lord, no. Remember, Max, remember.

"The last time we met," I say, my voice thick with emotion, "you know, before you showed up at my magazine, you almost got me arrested for prostitution."

West pulls back. "I'm sorry, I did what now?"

I huff out an unamused laugh. "Three years ago. You guys did a concert at the Forum. Afterward, some friends and I were looking for our car and we found you guys outside a back entrance. You called us over. Started to flirt. God, I was so stupidly flattered. I'd worshipped you for more than ten years. Then some cops came by. And I think …" I blink hard, fighting back tears of anger this time, all of the guilt evaporating as the memories pour back in, "in hindsight I think you were just trying to keep them from realizing you were high or had drugs on you or whatever, but you told them I was a prostitute trying to get you to hire me. I got handcuffed and shoved into the back of a police car while you guys hightailed it out of there with your security team. I cried and begged and pleaded, trying to explain that I wasn't a hooker. I think they finally figured out what had happened, because they let me go with a warning. Or they didn't want to make a scene since my friends were freaking out the whole time. Either way, it was one of the most traumatic experiences of my life. And that's the night I lost all respect for you. Oh, and your band, who didn't bother correcting your wildly harmful and false accusation."

I grip the steering wheel, purposely not looking at him. Expecting him to say something. Anything. A denial. An explanation. An apology. But the exact thing he's been begging me to tell him got no response. Nothing.

The whole drive. He stayed silent. I kept looking ahead.

I broke the silence eventually, asking him where he lived. Quietly, he told me. And nothing more even as I dropped him off. Not even a goodbye.

11

So What by Pink

West

I'm an asshole. Wait, what's worse than being an asshole? Because that's what I am. A lowlife piece-of-shit addict with a knack for destruction. My own life. My band. Other people's lives. I don't discriminate. I'll burn them all to the ground.

It doesn't matter that I care now. It doesn't matter that I'm not using anymore. It doesn't matter that the band is back together or that I've made a couple of stupid apologies. It doesn't change anything. My regret changes nothing. How do you unburn a bridge?

Obviously, my thoughts have spiraled since Maxi's revelation. In light of the horrifically awful

way I behaved toward someone who revered me …
well, it all feels futile. Some misdeeds are too heinous
to be forgiven. So why bother apologizing? What's it
fixing, really?

Oh yeah. My career. That.

It's the last thing I have. The only thing. If I can
salvage it, maybe the rest won't matter. At least, that's
what I tell myself. I have to. I have to have *something*
I can focus on that *can* be fixed. And as much as I
hate it, I've been given a road to follow to make that
happen. So I'm going to fucking follow it and take
what's coming to get at least that back.

Addiction may have completely changed the
course of my life, but I won't let it take music from
me. Or any fans still willing to see past a bunch of
drug-and-alcohol-fueled bad decisions. I have to
believe there are enough of them left to make this
worth it.

I heave a sigh as my driver speeds down the
freeway toward my next life implosion. Toward Sadie.
Another woman who hates me for good reason.

But when we pull up at a strip club, all I can do is
laugh. Looks like not much has changed, because this
is exactly where we met.

As soon as I step out of the car, as if I'm searching
for her, my eyes land on Maxi. I can tell by the tension
in her body, the hard set of her jaw, and how hard

she's gripping her takeaway coffee cup that she is not a happy camper. And while I would usually immediately think of all the ways I could tease her for it, today I feel *bad*. Jesus Christ.

In this moment, I know everything has changed. I saw her as the enemy before, the driving force behind this public lesson in humiliation and groveling. But knowing why she carries such hatred toward me? I can only accept the blame. I can't make it right. She doesn't want me to. But I can stop baiting her at every turn. Stop trying to get a rise out of her.

It's going to be hard. Because damned if it isn't fun watching her react.

As if she hears me thinking about torturing her, her head turns, and we lock eyes. And something lurches inside of me in a way that makes me wonder for the first time if I feel something more for her than dislike or regret.

Fuck. I think I respect Maxi Marshall.

Christ, I do. The woman is here. Though snarky, she's doing this. How could I not respect that?

I approach carefully, given our epically awful last conversation.

"Hey," I offer.

One of her dark, slender eyebrows raises. "Hi?"

I open my mouth to apologize, but snap it shut. How stupid would an apology be? *I'm sorry I almost got you arrested for prostitution, but I understand now why you'll always hate me?*

"So, your ex is a stripper, huh?" she asks, saving me from pulling together an apology I don't have the first clue how to make and sound sincere.

I shove my hands in my pocket and nod. "This is where we met, actually."

She rolls her eyes and I smile a little. And for some reason, my body relaxes.

"I guess I shouldn't be surprised by that," she murmurs, taking a sip of coffee.

"A little late in the day for caffeine, isn't it?" I offer lamely. *Christ, West.*

She snorts. "Thanks, Dad."

I shake my head, not wanting to banter back like I usually would. "Whatever. So, what's the plan? You guys aren't leaving me alone with her like you did with Erik, are you?"

A wicked smile spreads over Maxi's full, red lips. "Are you *afraid* of your ex, West?"

I shrug. "You would be too if you knew her."

That gets a full laugh out of her. "I met her a few minutes ago. She's gotta be a hundred pounds soaking wet." She eyes me up and down. "Pretty sure you could take her."

I scoff. "How little you know me. I'd never fight a woman, Maxi. Not even one as pretty as you." And with a wink, I decide to leave it there and find some-place else to be.

I make to head into the club, but one of Carter's assistants stops me at the door. "Sorry, Mr. Westberg, we're not ready for you yet."

I frown at him but raise my hands and back up. But when I turn around, Maxi's close behind, smirking at me.

"Hoping to get a lap dance while you're here?" she asks dryly.

I cock an eyebrow. "Why, are you offering?" I want to take the words back as soon as they're out, but verbally sparring with Maxi is second nature now.

She pulls a face. "Um. No." Then she takes a too-quick sip of coffee. But it doesn't stop me from seeing how red her face turns. Interesting.

"Don't worry, I'm not into chicks who'd be happier if I spontaneously combusted," I assure her.

Maxi throws up a hand. "For the last time, I don't hate you," she responds, sounding exasperated. "That would require —"

"Feeling something. Yeah, I've heard that song and dance before, Maxi. I'm starting to think you're saying it to convince *yourself*."

She props her free hand on her hip. "And what exactly does that mean?"

I sigh heavily, mostly frustrated with myself as I close the gap between us, so we're not overheard.

I stop directly in front of her, leaning in and catching her eye. The intensity between us skyrockets as soon as her hazel eyes meet mine.

"It means you have every right to *feel* something toward me, Maxi. Hate. Dislike. Anger. Whatever. But please, stop pretending I didn't completely shatter your trust. I deserve it. I deserve whatever you've got to throw at me. And you deserve to let it out. Whenever you want to do that, I'll listen. And afterward I'll still be as fucking sorry about what happened as I am right now. You have no fucking clue how sorry I am. I wish I could take it back, but I can't. But please, for the love of Christ, stop pretending like I didn't hurt you."

Maxi stares back at me in shock, her mouth hanging open.

"Mr. Westberg, Ms. Marshall, we're ready for you now," Carter's assistant calls from behind me.

And when I turn back to Maxi, she's already skirted around me to head into the club, leaving me to wonder if she really heard me or if she's going to continue avoiding her very real feelings toward me forever.

With a shake of my head, I head in after her. Carter is just inside.

"I hope you're already rolling because shit's going to get real, fast," I tell him.

Carter's brows hop up and he turns and nods to his assistant. Maxi pops up on my other side just as they indicate they're recording.

They have us sit in the club's waiting area on sticky baby blue vinyl couches.

"So, West, we're here today to see Sadie Sullivan, the woman you were dating right before rehab. How are you feeling?"

I try hard not to reply with a snarky comment. But I'm getting pretty sick of being asked how I'm feeling about everything all the time. Because trust me, they don't want the truth.

"Well, Sadie's a firecracker, so I've gotta admit that I'm a little nervous."

"Did you two not leave things on a good note?" she presses.

I can't help the skeptical look I give her. She must know. Everyone knows.

"Seeing as the last time we were together we were arrested for fucking on a theme park ride, in full view of the public, I'm going to go with no, we didn't leave things on a good note."

"That was the day you were busted for possession with intent to distribute, wasn't it?"

I huff an unamused laugh. "I still don't get why

they think one couple couldn't do all that coke," I reply jokingly.

Maxi frowns. Oof. Not winning any awards for cute here.

"Yes," I follow up. "It was the last straw, as far as the legal system was concerned. That was when I was given the choice between jail and rehab."

"Was it part of the court order for you to stay away from Sadie?"

I shake my head. "That just happened. I wasn't allowed visitors in rehab for the first month, and by the time I was … I dunno. I guess I thought it was best to just let her go." Best for my sobriety, that is, but I don't voice that part.

"But you were in a relationship for two years, correct?"

I nod my confirmation, though I wouldn't exactly call it a relationship. Intoxicated fucking is more like it. Sadie loved to fuck. She loved the drugs. And she really loved being with someone famous. But she didn't love me. And I didn't love her either, for that matter.

"Wow. So you pretty much left her hanging," Maxi says.

I fight the glare I want to shoot her. But I guess I deserve her judgment, more so than anyone's.

I spread my hands in surrender. "That's why we're here today, right?"

"Right," Maxi says softly. "Are you ready?"

I rise. "As I'll ever be."

Carter's assistant scrambles forward to show me into the club proper as the camera follows. Since they just opened, thankfully only a few people are at tables, mostly up against the stage. But the assistant, whose name I clearly never remember, veers to the right almost immediately, and I know exactly where he's taking us.

A private room. One that normally entertains every manner of debauchery, much of which Sadie and I engaged in here ourselves. And my suspicion that they brought us here for the mere spectacle of flesh and sex is pretty much confirmed. These places never let people bring cameras in, yet here we are, about to film in one of the most private locations they offer.

At least there's a camera rolling to keep Sadie from actually murdering me.

"I'll be here the whole time," he assures me, making me wonder if Maxi managed to say something to him.

Or maybe the management here required we not be left alone in a room together with just a camera. That makes me laugh.

The assistant knocks and I'm suddenly wishing I'd worn a cup. Or anything that'll protect my balls when Sadie decides to try ripping them off.

"Come in," a female voice calls.

The assistant opens the door and gestures for me to enter. I walk in and they follow. And there she is. All five-feet-six-inches of Sadie in all her platform-heeled, curled-blond hair, shiny pink-lipped, barely-there cowgirl outfit glory.

"West," she cries, throwing herself into my arms.

I'm so caught off guard, I let her, and the camera moves around us to capture the reunion.

"Nice to see you too, Sadie." Well. Maybe this won't be as bad as I thought.

I pry her off me as subtly as I can. And as soon as she's away, she reels back one arm and smacks me so hard my head twists to the side.

"Holy shit," I cry. "What the hell?"

"That's for never breaking up with me, asshole," she yells. Then she *pushes* me.

But just as Maxi pointed out, she's tiny, so it barely registers. Once she realizes that, she swings out with a leg. I attempt to dodge it, but she gets me in the shin with the sharp tip of her heel and I lean to the side, pulling the weight off my leg in reaction to the pain.

"And that's for getting me arrested," she spits.

"Okay, I get it, I'm sorry, Sadie. Really. Jesus. You can stop now," I cry, throwing up a hand when I see her coming back at me.

"Oh, I'm just getting started," she says, making to knee me in the groin.

But I push her knee aside with one hand before she can connect. She topples backward into me, but not content to be thwarted, she reaches up with her clawlike nails as she falls, grabbing at my face.

I hear the assistant calling for security as I dart into a corner and she rights herself.

"I'm not here to fight," I assure her, holding my hand up and hobbling from the injury to my shin.

"Then you shouldn't have come," Sadie hisses.

She lashes out with a fist that I grab, spinning her around and holding her back against my front, her arms locked in mine, rendering her helpless. Unfortunately, my starved dick likes it more than I do, and she knows it, grinding against me. With a hiss, I release her and she spins away, facing me and looking like she's trying to figure out where to strike next.

"You were there too," I remind her. "Nobody forced drugs on you. That's what we did, Sadie, it's who we were together. But I'm not that guy anymore. And I'm sorry if I hurt you, but you have to stop now."

She screams like an animal and launches herself at

me just as a huge security guard catches her by the waist. She wriggles and screams against him.

"Fuck you, West. FUCK! YOU!" she screams. "You ruined my life that day. I will never forgive you. *Never!*"

The security guard hauls her out, only to be replaced by an older man. "I think you guys should leave," he huffs. "Hope you got what you came for."

ABOUT HALF AN HOUR LATER, AFTER CARTER'S CREW has pulled out of the strip club, I find myself sitting on a bench with the club in the background, waiting for Maxi to do the post interview. I've already checked myself for damage — there's just one scratch along my jawline to go with the painful bruise on my shin — now I just need to calm myself down.

"I watched the footage. You weren't wrong about her." Maxi's voice suddenly behind me startles me so much I jump a little. She settles on the bench next to me. "Sorry, didn't mean to scare you."

I give her a small smile. "Not your fault. I'm a little on edge right now."

She nods understandingly. "I don't blame you. God, what a vindictive bitch to use an opportunity where you were going to apologize to physically attack you. I won't even ask why. She's clearly got issues. But I think the real question is, are you okay?"

"You're concerned about me?" I ask, shaking my head in disbelief.

"I'm … yes. I'm concerned. And I'm angry. And disappointed. And hurt," she admits, twisting her fingers together. "But I also feel guilty. I don't want to be any of those things at you. Maybe because deep down I know what addiction does to a person, and that I'm blaming you when I should be blaming the disease."

"I made the choices that led me there," I reply. "But thank you for saying that."

"Are you sure you're okay?" she asks skeptically.

I look at her. Really look at her. Her luscious, wavy hair. Her rocker chick band T-shirt style — today it's The Who. But mostly I look at her and think about the things you can't see. Just like you can't see addiction, Maxi doesn't show her pain either. But I know it's there. And knowing I caused it sucks balls.

"Yeah, I'm fine, thanks. Are we fine, Maxi?"

She huffs a sigh out of her nose. "Look, I know I've become some kind of metaphor for you earning forgiveness. But you don't need me to forgive you, West. I'm nobody to you. There is no 'we.' Yes, what you did hurt me, but I'm a big girl. I've been dealing with it for years, and I'll continue to."

"Is that a fancy way of saying you won't forgive me?"

She twists her fingers faster. "I hear your apology. And I appreciate it. I don't know. I *want* to forgive you. I'm just not there yet."

"That's fair," I admit.

She looks up at me. "Did Sadie knock the sass out of you? You're being so calm and mature."

I laugh. "Maybe." I shrug.

"Dude, seriously. You haven't made fun of me once this whole conversation. This is weird."

"It is a little weird, isn't it?"

Now it's her turn to laugh. "Glad it's not just me."

Carter and crew show up, starting to set up their equipment for the post-apology interview. But before we get there, I can't let one thing she said go unchallenged.

"Maxi?"

"Hm?"

"You're not nobody to me. Not even close."

12

In Between by Linkin Park

Max

After our strange conversation outside of the strip club, my biggest concern was that when we flew to San Francisco, I'd have to sit with West. I have no idea what to say to him right now. I don't even know what I think about everything he said yet.

Thankfully, I ended up taking an earlier flight to do some legwork with Alexsis. Giving me time to unpack what his words made me feel.

He said everything I'd ever wanted to hear from him and more. But instead of feeling vindicated, I'm more confused than ever. So here I am, sitting in coach, talking to Alexsis about it.

"Maybe it's because you spent the last three years pretending you didn't hate him," she offers. "That's a hard switch to just turn off."

"I didn't hate him," I protest. "Why does everyone think that? There's so much more wrapped up in what happened. I don't hate him, not at all. But I was angry. Am angry? I don't know. *That* is a hard switch to turn off."

"And you don't have to. Just because he's got a sudden pathological need to be forgiven doesn't mean you're expected to magically get over it."

"Thank you," I tell her. "I definitely feel that pressure. But you're right. I don't have to. Let's talk about something else. How are things going with Ford?"

Alexsis pulls a face. "Eh. After the first date magic wore off — okay, maybe second or third date — I realized you were right. He's a pompous asshole."

I heave a comical sigh of relief. "Well thank god you figured that out on your own."

"I guess. I just don't get it. There were sparks! And he had so much promise. Why does it have to be so hard to find a decent guy?" she groans. "I mean, how many frogs do I have to kiss for fuck's sake?"

I chuckle. "You're asking the wrong girl. There's a reason I don't date more. At some point it becomes a chore, and you just have to back off and realize your life is pretty fucking awesome as it is."

Alexsis tilts her head. "You know what? You're right. I graduated college. I'm a journalist at a rock magazine. I'm traveling to — er, not-so-exotic but still cool locations."

"San Francisco *is* cool. And maybe after we get this apology shoot we can go out and see some sights before we head home."

"I'm down with that," she agrees. "Speaking of the shoot. We should start spitballing locations since the owner of the café the sister wants to meet at isn't on board."

"Okay, what have you got?"

She opens her laptop and pulls up a marked map. "Café is here," she says, pointing. Then shifting her finger a bit to the right. "There's a public park nearby."

I shake my head. "You don't know the full story behind this apology," I realize.

"I guess not. But why does that affect the shoot location?" she asks, puzzled.

"Trust me. We don't want this one public. Can we just get a suite at the hotel? Something with a living room?" I muse.

"That could work. I'll get on it when we check in."

"Perfect. Thanks, Alexsis. You know. For listening."

She gives me a funny half-smile. "Anytime. When you realize you still have the hots for West, I want to listen to that too."

I roll my eyes. "Ha! Don't hold your breath."

Despite what I said to Alexsis, her comment triggered something in me. Something I didn't realize until we met up with West in the living room of his suite, which we've decided to use for the shoot. But as soon as we walked in for our pre-apology prep and interviewing, I knew. I knew she was right.

The sight of him pacing. Running his hands through his thick, dark hair. The intensity. It's exactly what he does on stage. What I've personally watched him do on stage more times than I can count, granted usually with Rosie hanging from a strap around his neck. But it's that intensity that always drew me to him. The dark, pulsing energy that rolls off him in waves. It's like a magnet.

I should hate this guy for all eternity. But I don't. What is wrong with me? Do I have a savior complex? Perhaps, though I don't think that's the appeal for me. While part of West's draw has always been the tortured bad-boy angle, I've seen firsthand now that he's not bad. But he is troubled. And while I don't think for a minute anything I could do would fix him, it's hard not to want to go wrap my arms around him.

But I don't do that. Instead, I stand frozen just inside the door, a realization hitting me like a ton of bricks: Forgiving him is like giving myself permission to remember the rock star I fell in love with from afar. Except now I know him up close. And he riles me in good and bad ways. But it's the good ways that worry me. Because I don't think I'd survive another Kristoffer Westberg heartbreak. And the bad ways? I have to admit, it's kind of exciting to spar with him verbally. I know he enjoys it. Maybe I do too.

He looks up and catches my eye. I suddenly feel naked, like he can see every thought that was passing through my mind. As he continues to hold my gaze, the feeling intensifies, until Carter grabs his attention to discuss logistics.

Before I'm prepared, I'm pulled in for the pre-interview. West and I take a seat on the couch while they finalize lighting.

"Hey," I offer lamely. "So this is going to be a tough one. You ready?"

"More than you know. I'm just so fucking relieved they got her to agree to come here. I don't even care if they paid her to do it," he admits.

My brows bunch together. "You didn't think she would?"

He gives me a look. "I already told you where she's at. She knows what I want. I've been trying to get her to talk to me for more than a year, but she's refused all contact."

"I don't think they paid her," I offer. "Maybe she was just ready this time."

He shakes his head. "I'd like to believe that, but I was here a month ago and nothing had changed. I'm just bracing myself for the possibility that she's not coming for the reasons I hope she is."

The anguish on his face gets to me, and before I can think about it, I reach out and squeeze his hand reassuringly. I have no words to offer. What do I know about his sister or their relationship? The least I can do is offer comfort.

He gives me a smile I haven't seen before. His eyes are warm, his mouth tilted up on one side. He squeezes back and my heart flutters. I'm so screwed.

"Okay, we're ready," Carter calls.

I pull back self-consciously and give thoughts of West's smile a giant shove out of my brain. Time to focus on the task at hand.

———𝄞———

WE FINISH THE PRE-INTERVIEW AND THE WAIT BEGINS. But the time his sister was supposed to arrive has come and gone. As time passes, whatever small bursts of conversation were happening cease. Carter regularly checks with the driver who was supposed to pick her up. He's there, she's just not answering the door, or her phone.

Just when we're about to give up nearly two hours later, there's a knock on the door. Carter's assistant answers and we hear a strangled cry.

"Kris?" a woman's voice calls.

West, who'd been sitting on the couch, head in hands, looks up in surprise and quickly bolts to the door.

"Annika?" he returns. And then a broken sob rips out of him as he draws the tiny female at the door into his arms.

Carter has his assistant swing the camera toward them, but something inside me protests.

"Carter?" I call softly. He looks at me. I point to the camera and shake my head. He pulls a face. "Turn it off."

With a small sigh, he complies.

West leads his sister into the room and one look at her tells me my instincts were dead-on. A massive bruise covers her right eye and part of her face. She has scratches on her neck. And she looks deflated. Like she's hit rock bottom.

West settles her on the couch and I get his attention. He steps to the side where she can't hear.

"We don't have to film this," I tell him. "Say the word and I'll get everyone out of here."

West closes his eyes for a moment, his shoulders dropping with relief. He reopens them, his eyes now glistening, and simply says, "Thank you."

I swallow hard and nod, quickly working to usher everyone out. "Call me when you're ready."

He nods, and I leave with the last of the crew. The last thing I see as I close the door behind me is him crouched in front of his shaking, beaten little sister.

NEARLY SIX HOURS LATER, JUST AFTER TEN, THERE'S A soft knock on my hotel room door. I keep the bolt closed and open the door a crack to find West leaning against the doorframe.

"Can I come in?" he asks, his voice hoarse.

I close the door, unlatch the bolt, and reopen it. "Of course," I reply, gesturing for him to enter. Trying not to be self-conscious of my sweats and "Peace, Love, & Music" Snoopy T-shirt.

He tugs on the hem of my shirt as he passes. "Cute," he murmurs with a small, tired smile.

"Thanks," I reply, closing the door.

He settles on the small, utilitarian navy couch

across from the bed. No private living room here. The only other furniture is a dresser on the wall between them. I take a seat next to him, which is as far away as the loveseat will allow.

"How'd it go?" I ask.

He scrubs his hands over his face. "You were right. She was ready. The bastard beat her when she told him she was going to see me today. She had to wait until he was gone to leave. She won't be going back."

"Is she still using?" I ask.

West shakes his head. "No, thank god. Apparently she got pregnant a year or so ago and stopped. She still lost the baby, but she hasn't gone back. At least, not to the hard stuff."

"Well, that's a relief. So she finally wanted to leave?"

He tips his head back and forth. "She wasn't sure how she could, so I told her to take my room. For as long as she needs, I'll make sure she has a place to stay away from him. I tried to get her to come home, but she's afraid of everything right now, especially our dad."

"Sounds like there's a lot of that going around. But I guess I'll get to see firsthand why that is soon."

"I'm sorry I threw us off today. Is Carter pissed?"

I look up at him in shock. "Fuck Carter," I reply

vehemently. "If he couldn't look at your sister and see that doing a fucking interview was the last thing she needed, then he's a fucking waste of space."

"Wow, Maxi, that was more cursing in one breath than I've ever heard out of your mouth," he teases. Then he leans in. "I like it."

I snort. "You would appreciate a foul mouth."

"No. Well, yes, but that's not what I meant. I like that you get what's important. It's something I'm still learning. I think you're a good influence, though, Maxi. I may keep you around a while."

I scrunch my nose. "You get me for …" I quickly calculate how many days between now and the airing party. "About three weeks. Though I doubt we'll need to see each other much during post."

"Well, that's a shame."

I shrug. "So you dropped by to let me know your sister is okay?"

He sinks into the couch a little, clearly exhausted, leaning his head back and stretching out his legs. "Yep. And to ask what my penance will be. Then I'll go get another room."

"Carter plans to do post in the morning before we leave." I pause. "And we also planned to do the shoot in your suite because we couldn't get another room; the hotel's fully booked. So you can just stay here."

He opens his eyes and looks up at me. "Well, fuck,

Maxi. A pretty girl asks you to sleep over, you can't say no. But I don't have to. I can go crash with Carter or something."

I roll my eyes. "I have a king-sized bed, there's plenty of room, and we're both adults. Besides, you don't even like Carter and you look like you're about to fall asleep right there." As if to prove my point, his eyes had drifted close in the middle of my rant, and they now pop back open.

"You're a saint, Maxi."

I snort, rising and heading to my side of the bed. "Hardly." I point at the side I wasn't planning on sleeping on. "You can take that side. Consider it your reward for doing right by your sister today."

With a sleepy smile, he rises, kicks off his shoes, then falls face-first on top of the covers. And I'm pretty sure he falls right to sleep.

Me? I lay on my side of the bed wondering what form of temporary insanity caused me to invite West into my bed. Even if it's not like *that*. Sometimes I'm too nice for my own good. Or, as Alexsis would probably say, it's just a sign of all the "secret" feelings I have for West. Well, news flash, Alexsis, they're not secret. I've just learned to ignore them for a very long time.

I WAKE IN THE MIDDLE OF THE NIGHT FOR ABSOLUTELY no reason at all. The room is eerily quiet, but now that I'm awake, I realize … I really need to use the bathroom. I debate for a good few minutes, not wanting to chance waking West.

I glance over my shoulder to find him lying on his back, though still on top of the covers, but he's perfectly still. The longer I wait, the stronger the need becomes, so I finally give in.

I do my business as quietly as I can manage before creeping back to the bed as slowly and stealthily as possible.

"You can stop acting like a cat burglar. I'm awake," West says dryly.

"Shit, sorry," I mumble as I climb back into bed.

In the dim moonlight peeking around the drapes, I see him tilt his head toward me.

"It's not your fault. I never went to sleep."

I glance at the clock. It's almost two.

"Makes sense you'd be a night owl," I reply, wiggling to get comfortable.

"I'm actually fucking exhausted, but every time I close my eyes I see that bruise on Annika's face and I get pissed off all over again," he admits.

My heart twists. "I'd be angry at the fucker who did that to her too."

West rolls toward me, and I pull my head back in

surprise. He's still not super close, but the move makes me nervous for reasons I'm not willing to examine too closely.

"I'm the fucker who did that to her," he says ardently. "Or I might as well have. I introduced them. I introduced her to heroin, Maxi. Nobody else. This is on me."

I scoot up on my pillow. "How old was she then?"

His brows scrunch together. "Twenty-five. Why?"

"Because that means she was a grown woman, perfectly capable of making her own choices. That's not to say you didn't play a part; I'm just pointing out that it's not all on you."

He huffs a breath out of his nose in clear disbelief. "Annika's worshipped me since we were kids. She even wanted her own guitar when she was ten so she could be just like me. She's always wanted to be like me. This isn't on her. It was reckless, thoughtless, and totally fucking insane to bring her into that world." He shakes his head and flops backward onto his pillow.

I blink hard against tears as my heart bleeds for him. For Annika. For their family, and what both of their addictions have done to all of their lives.

"Did she forgive you?"

West shakes his head, and I'm surprised, until he says, "Yes. But I don't fucking deserve it."

"Nobody *deserves* forgiveness, West. They earn it. And I think you earned it today."

"Thanks," he murmurs, surprising me. I expected snark. Or at least more protest. He must really be twisted up over this. "Let's just hope Carter, Ford, and the rest of those fuckers think so too."

"Don't worry about that. I have some ideas for what we can shoot to cover our asses."

"Good. Because I'm all out of fucks to give." Every word is laced with exhaustion. The soul-deep, heartrending kind, and it's all I can do not to reach out and comfort him.

But touching him would be a very bad idea. So instead, I offer the only comfort I can think of.

"West?"

"Yeah?"

"For what it's worth? You've earned my forgiveness too."

I swallow hard against the conflicted emotions saying those words out loud brings. Because I really do forgive him. But I haven't forgotten yet. I'm not sure if I ever will.

West's head slowly rolls toward me. And though I can't see his eyes in the dark, I can feel them searching for mine. I close my eyes, the vulnerability of this moment too much to bear.

Really, though, how could I not forgive him? He's

crawled out of the pit of addiction and, despite understandable protests, is laying his life out in front of the masses while he attempts to make amends for the things he's done. That takes a strength of character I'm not sure many people have, myself included.

So as wary as I am of him, it's a truth I can't withhold. And one I'm pretty sure he needed to hear right now.

But the silence stretches on.

"You still awake?" I ask self-consciously.

A deep chuckle rumbles out of West. "I'm awake. I heard you. I just … I'm kinda shocked, to be honest, Maxi. Thought you'd take that grudge to the grave. Not that I'd blame you."

"Is that your way of saying thank you?" I ask wryly.

"Yeah. I guess it is."

I snort. "You're welcome, then. Get some sleep, West. You're going to need it."

He doesn't respond. But a few minutes later, I hear his breathing even out. I sit up delicately and carefully lean toward him. He's finally asleep.

I watch him for a moment, fighting that feeling that keeps grabbing me. The one that says this is all too unreal; that I'm the one sleeping, my subconscious creating this fantastical dream to resolve all the feelings I've had about this man over the years.

Except I know if it were me dreaming this, it would've been without all the snarky banter that makes me want to slap him. And there would have been a lot less clothing.

With a quiet chuckle, I roll over and allow myself to drift off, equal parts wanting and fearing to have those particular types of dreams about West again. But they're just dreams, right?

13

Father of Mine by Everclear

Max

Two days after San Francisco, we're back in Corona for West's apology to his father. And while I'm looking forward to finally understanding this piece of West's puzzle, I'm not looking forward to another awkward-as-ass encounter.

Because from the moment we woke up Friday morning, we had no clue how to behave around each other after the momentarily peaceful connection we'd shared in the wee hours of the night.

Those moments shook the foundations of our whole dynamic. And now what? Now awkwardness with a side of tongue-tied idiocy.

Because of which the first half of Friday was spent avoiding conversation during down moments while we recreated what happened between West and his sister with interviews — not including his sister, of course. The second half was travel, which none of us did together. Alexsis went back first thing, then me after interviews, then the crew after taking some scenic footage to cut in, with West staying behind another day to look after his sister. So I didn't even get to tell Alexsis what had happened, and she's not here today to act as a buffer. But thankfully I didn't have to travel with West. Half a day of trying to reestablish our rapport was more than enough.

But today will be a full day of just me, West, and Carter and crew. Oh, and Bill Westberg.

In an effort to find something to talk about, I tried asking West a bit about his relationship with his father on Friday morning, but he continued to stubbornly deflect talking about it. So I'm pretty much flying blind here. This ought to be fun.

I pull up outside of West's childhood home to find the production van already there, with Carter sifting through equipment in the back.

"Hey, Carter," I greet him.

His sandy blond head pops up and he adjusts his glasses. "Afternoon, Max. I'm glad you're here early." He sets some recording equipment down and takes a seat on the tailgate. "Ford and I had a meeting yesterday. He's happy with what he's seeing, but since we couldn't get the actual apology with the sister on camera, he wants to make sure this one packs an extra emotional punch. Plus it's the last before the private concert."

I frown, instantly knowing what he's asking. "You want me to push West's buttons before the interview."

Carter nods slowly. "Something like that. You seem to have a knack for it anyway."

I shake my head. "Except West has purposely kept me at arm's length on this one. I have nothing to go on. I wouldn't even know where to start."

Carter removes his glasses and starts cleaning them on his shirt. "Ah. Yes. Well. I may have had a bit of a chat with Erik Westberg that went beyond what we technically needed for the shoot."

I quirk an eyebrow. "About?"

"His sister and father. I wanted to be prepared."

"You know something," I accuse.

Carter nods grimly. "I know everything."

WEST BREEZES IN MINUTES BEFORE WE'D PLANNED TO start shooting. I know it's part of his attempt to keep me in the dark, but he's unknowingly already lost that advantage, courtesy of Erik and Carter.

"Maxi," West greets me with a curt nod. Not awkwardly, but definitely more reserved than usual.

It takes me a moment to realize his energy is *nervous*. And if I was unsure before, I'm dead certain now. I can't do what Carter and Ford want me to do.

"We need to talk," I respond, pulling at his arm and leading him to my car. "Get in."

He gives me a quizzical look but does as I ask. As soon as the doors are closed, I realize I don't even know how to begin.

"Are we going somewhere?" West asks.

I shake my head. "No." I take a deep breath. Here goes nothing. "They want me to push your buttons before you go in to talk to your dad."

West snorts. "What else is new? This whole charade is about pushing my buttons, isn't it?"

I press my lips together in frustration.

"This is worse. So much worse."

"Worse how?"

I pause, not wanting to reveal his brother's role in this. No sense shaking that tree. Might as well let him assume it came from his father. Lord knows West kept them well away from his sister, so he'll know she wasn't the one to spill the beans.

"They know everything, West," I say carefully.

"And they want me to tell you in the pre-interview that your father has had professional help and is — their words — a different man now. They want to see you break down. They want you two to reconcile on camera. And they want you both crying."

West pales. "Do *you* know everything?" he asks somberly.

And the anxiety written all over his face, in his voice, makes my heart shatter.

But before I can respond, someone knocks on the window behind West's head, startling us both.

He pops the door open to reveal Carter.

"We're ready," Carter says abruptly before walking away.

With the door still propped open, West looks back at me.

"You don't have to do this," I tell him.

His jaw clenches. "Let's go, Maxi."

"Wait," I call.

But he's already out of the car.

So, with seemingly no other choice, I join him.

Carter has cameras set up on the front walkway, clearly intending to shoot with the house behind us. His assistant lines us up on our marks.

And then we're rolling. For the first time, I may be just as uneasy as West is.

"We're here outside of the Westberg family home,

getting ready to talk to your dad," I say, looking toward West. "How are you feeling right now, West?"

"Just peachy, Maxi, thanks for asking," he replies drolly.

"Really?" I press. "Because from what I understand, your dad wasn't the nicest guy to you as a teenager."

"Nope," he confirms brightly.

And his perky yet sarcastic responses are unnerving me even more.

"You left home at sixteen because of his abuse, didn't you?" I continue, trying to get us to the end of this line of questioning with my sanity intact.

"Sure did," he agrees just as peppily as before.

"But," I start, swallowing hard against the lump forming in my throat at what I have to say next, "your mom died giving birth to your sister. So he went it alone as a parent. That must have made it hard for him. Hard for everyone, really."

It's a softer version of what they wanted me to say, but right now all I want is real emotion from West. Not the bullshit face he's putting on to get through this, even though I don't blame him for it.

"It was hard. But you know, what's done is done." He shrugs.

I suppress a sigh. This is going nowhere. "So, for your part, what are you apologizing for today, West?"

"Well, I sure didn't make it easy on him," West replies, appearing thoughtful, but I know him better now. And right now I can completely smell the bullshit. "I was rebellious from a young age. He wanted me to go into a 'serious' career, not music. I started drinking and smoking at twelve. So, you know, any parent would be upset about that."

I have to give him credit. To someone who didn't know him, it would sound genuine.

"Sure. But he's admitted to having behaved … poorly," I say, stumbling for the right word. "He's even had therapy and is supposedly a changed man. Kind of like you."

West's gaze lands on mine sharply, a muscle in his jaw ticking. And I know instantly that the comparison gets to him.

"I guess we'll see," is his only response.

And I'm honestly impressed by his self-control.

I nod in agreement. "I guess so. Because it's time for a father-son reunion."

As soon as the cameras stop, West walks away from me.

I watch his back retreat helplessly as Carter approaches.

"That was not exactly what we were looking for," Carter admonishes me.

"I can't out him on television, Carter."

"You mean you *won't*," Carter clarifies.

I roll my eyes. "Fine, I won't. But it's West's past. If it's coming from anyone, it has to come from him."

Carter considers me for a moment. "Fine. As long as we get the waterworks, I can't say I care. But it would make for great ratings."

It's all I can do not to punch him, but thankfully West rejoins us and I'm distracted out of my anger as one of the assistants explains how the next shot will go.

And then, once more, it's showtime.

For the first time since the beginning, I can't help feeling like it really is all just for show.

With cameras trained on us, I reach up and knock.

The door swings open too quickly for West's dad to not have been standing there, waiting.

"Kristoffer," his dad gasps. And I can see real emotion on his face, at least.

"Hi, Dad," West offers dully.

Bill Westberg launches forward, pulling West into a hug. My eyes go wide and I hold my breath, waiting for West to shove his father off of him.

But while he's stiff, I have to give West credit for allowing it much more than I'd expected. He does somewhat awkwardly pat his father on the back until he lets go.

"Come in," Bill offers, stepping back and allowing us over the threshold.

The exterior cameras stop as they get us set up quickly in the living room, just inside the door past a small entryway. The house is sparsely decorated, with barely more than utilitarian furniture. In a word, it's depressing. And maybe it's just what I know, but being in the house gives me the heebie-jeebies.

Thankfully with just a few minutes, a little makeup, and some lighting adjustments later have us rolling again. That much closer to getting the hell out of here.

"So, you know why we're here, Mr. Westberg," I offer from the lone armchair.

West sits on one end of the three-person couch, his father on the other.

"Yes, but please, call me Bill," he says warmly.

I take him in fully for the first time. He looks so much like West, except his eyes are blue. And, of course, he's a good twenty-five years older, with gray sprinkling through the dark brown of his hair, and fine lines at the edges of his eyes and lips when he smiles.

I try my best to shove my own judgments aside and simply do my job.

"Bill," I respond. "How long has it been since you've seen your son?"

"Twenty years," he responds. "Twenty long years."

"And though it may go without saying, you two didn't part on the best of terms," I prompt.

"No," his dad agrees. "I was hard on Kris. I knew he was talented, but I wanted more for him than being a struggling artist."

"Except he wasn't," I point out before I can stop myself. "Not for long, anyway."

Bill shrugs lightly. "The odds weren't in his favor. Surely you can understand that, as a parent, I had to be honest with him about that."

"That's fair," I agree. "But that wasn't all the blowup was about, was it?"

It's as close as I'm willing to skate to the issue.

Bill clears his throat. "No. I had … other issues. But I've gotten help," he says, now turning to West, his eyes glistening. "Without your mom here, I lost my way. And I'm sorry, son. I hope you can forgive me."

My eyes flick to West, and I'm surprised to see the similar sheen of unshed tears in his eyes. West shakes his head, something I'm realizing is a habit, and not necessarily indicative of what he's about to say.

"I don't know. Can you forgive me for being such a disappointment?" There's a bitterness to his words that rings with truth.

"Oh, Kris." His dad says, a sob catching in his throat. "You were never a disappointment to me."

West blows out a breath and simply nods, wiping at his face as a tear starts to fall. Bill leans forward and offers a hug to West, who reluctantly allows it. Bill's head is turned toward the camera, and there's no mistaking the tears streaming down his cheeks.

I glance back at Carter to find his eyes fixed on the pair, smiling happily. It makes me angry, but at least he's getting what he wants. Hopefully that means this farce can come to a quick end.

And it does. With a few more platitudes from me, a bit more fatherly blubbering from Bill, and the barest of responses from West, we wrap.

West rises, visibly shaking, while the crew starts to move back outside for post.

He makes to walk by me, out of the living room, but I reach a hand out and touch his arm. He pauses, looking down at me.

"You okay?" I ask quietly.

He shakes his head tightly. "Get everyone out. Now."

My eyes go wide, but I get Carter to hurry and within a couple of minutes, we're headed out the door.

"I'll be out in a minute," West says, following me to the door. His expression brooks no questions, so I simply leave.

The sound of the door closing behind me sends shivers down my spine. As much as I don't want to leave West alone, I know that's what he wants right now. So I join the production crew at the edge of the property again, standing in for camera adjustments. Thankfully, based on Carter's comments, he's as pleased as he seemed inside. The whole situation just makes me sick.

When I hear the front door open and close behind me, I whirl toward it. West is walking down the steps, flexing his hand.

My heart drops, knowing what he most likely just did. Not that I can blame him. If my father had done what his had, I'd have left home too. And if I'd been forced to "apologize" to him twenty years later? I'd punch him too. Probably more.

Even more surprising, West makes it through the post interview perfectly, showing no hint how upset I know he must be.

I'm left in awe of West. And of his father's audacity. Because what kind of father — nay, *human being* — abuses their own children and then thinks he can just move on? Because it was not just the occasional kind of verbal abuse we all endure growing up. It was physically, beating his children to the point of broken bones. Mentally, gaslighting them on all their forms of abuse to convince them it was all in their minds.

Emotionally, by making them feel worthless. And, most horrifically, from ages too young to even fathom, abusing them sexually at length, often in front of each other as punishment.

I don't care what bullshit Bill Westberg spouted in that house. People that depraved don't magically change. And I also don't care what West said; I know he hasn't forgiven his father. His years of drug abuse make sense now. Who wouldn't want to forget all of that?

But moreover, who could ever truly forgive someone who did that to them?

Another concern follows me home: Will West forgive *me* for playing a part in today? Because I feel disgusted with myself.

I also feel angry on West's behalf. Not just at his father, but at Carter, Ford, Burke, and everyone else who wants to drag him through this travesty for the sake of entertainment and ticket sales. I don't know why West is tolerating it, but the fact that he is doesn't absolve me of my role in it.

My only small comfort is that today's shoot with his father was the last personal apology. The private fan event will be a cakewalk in comparison. I can only hope that, in the end, the apology tour is really worth it. But that's West's call, not mine. And based on his participation today, I can only assume he thinks it is.

But then, he's had his dignity stripped from him his whole life. Maybe he's too used to it. Maybe I'm the odd one out for thinking he deserves better. Because he does. Underneath all of the drug use, the mistakes, there was someone hurting. Someone who is now trying to atone for … well, being human.

I, like so many others, thought more about how he'd disappointed me rather than how life had disappointed him. And hopefully, like me, everyone else will see how very wrong they were.

14

With or Without You by U2

West

"Let the insanity begin," Ward declares magnanimously, spreading his arms wide. "I'll just be backstage."

He winks and ducks offstage, not waiting for a response. I shake my head and walk out of the stage pit, up to the greeting area we've set up by the bar.

Nils, the manager for the club, Baltia, meets me at the main table. Dude could be Ward's long-lost twin brother with his tall, thin frame and blond hair. Minus Ward's tattoos, though.

"Need anything else?" he asks.

"Nope. Frankie's not gonna be here tonight?" I ask.

Nils shakes his head. "Her and her husband are having a birthday party for their one-year-old first thing in the morning."

I laugh. Frankie Greco married with a kid. Stranger things have happened, I guess. "Well, say hi to her for me."

Nils nods. "Will do. It's good to see you healthy, man."

I slug him playfully on the arm. "Thanks. It feels good to be healthy. And thanks for hosting this on such short notice."

He shrugs. "You know we've always got your back. Besides, you were one of Baltia's first acts back when Frankie redid the place. It's the least we can do."

I make to respond when I notice Maxi walk in, her assistant in tow. It's been five days since I saw her at my dad's house. And I'm no less conscious of what she knows about me. But somehow, I'm still glad to see her. Maybe it has something to do with the fact that she's more dressed up than I've ever seen her in a tight black strapless number and red heels, her hair still tumbling in waves over her shoulder, her lips painted red to match her shoes. Jesus fucking Christ, she's hot.

"Hey, Maxi," I greet her as she approaches, shamelessly staring at her. I gesture to Nils. "This is Nils, Baltia's manager."

Maxi's assistant, Alexsis claps a hand over her mouth. "Oh my god, Nils Larssen?!"

I smirk, knowing Nils was once a runway model. So he's probably just as used to the groupies as the acts he books are.

She waves her hands in excitement. "You don't remember me, do you?" she asks him.

Maxi and I exchange a bewildered look.

"I'm sorry, I don't," Nils says. "You are …?"

"Alexsis Monaghan," she squeals, then turns to Maxi. "Nils was an exchange student who stayed with us … oh my gosh, what was it? Fifteen years ago?"

"Holy shit," Nils gasps, his eyes now trailing over Alexsis. "Seventeen years ago. You were a baby. What, five years old? I'm surprised you even remember me. Now look at you." And boy does he look at her.

Not that I blame him. I hadn't paid much attention because Maxi was there, but Alexsis is wearing a red halter dress that looks painted on her ample curves. She's a little short for my taste. And a little blonde. But then, I guess I'm just a sucker for a brunette. My eyes flick to Maxi at the thought to find her staring at me, which makes me smirk. Which, in turn, makes her roll her eyes.

I chuckle, coming back to reality.

"Are you kidding? You were my first crush," she tells him, batting her eyelashes.

And now *I* roll my eyes. I catch Maxi's eye and cock my head to the side, inviting her to step away with me. She nods and we slip away. Nils and Alexsis don't even notice.

"Well, that was cute," Maxi says.

I huff a laugh. "Small world, I guess."

"So, you ready for tonight?"

I lift a shoulder. "As I'll ever be. Ford's sending a photographer. You'll be documenting the awesomeness. Club's providing muscle in case any of the fans get crazy."

"Or handsy," Maxi mutters.

I grin. "Not jealous, are you?"

She rolls her eyes. "Oh, please," she scoffs.

The normality of sparring with her calms me somehow.

"Well, if you want an autograph too, all you have to do is say so," I tease, stopping at the table and gesturing at the stack of photos waiting to be signed.

"I'll keep that in mind," she replies dryly.

"You do that," I reply with a wink. "You're sticking around for the concert, right?"

"Of course. Part of the job." She shifts feet. "West?"

"Maxi?"

"Are you … upset with me? For Sunday?" She blushes bright red, and I don't think I've ever seen my feisty little journalist so self-conscious.

"No, Maxi. We were all just playing our parts. I appreciate that you tried not to blindside me, actually."

She nods but still looks unconvinced. "Okay. I just … I felt bad. It was just all … badness."

I snort. "Truer words never spoken. And water under the bridge. Let's get a drink, shall we?"

Maxi goes for the hard stuff, though for obvious reason I stick with seltzer water.

Before I know it, it's time for the meet and greet with the approximately five hundred fans selected. It sounds like a lot, but considering this place could comfortably hold twice that, it still feels intimate.

And it feels fucking good to be signing autographs, taking pictures, and making the fans happy. None of them are even angry, mostly expressing their concern for me and that they're glad the band is back together. Still, I do my best to play along and make apologies wherever they seem natural. It actually feels good.

But what feels fucking phenomenal is getting on

that stage and playing the shit out of our classics, plus a few of the new songs, and watching the crowd go nuts.

And what feels way better than it probably should is spotting Maxi in that crowd, front and center. Smiling, despite herself. I may play to her a little more than I want to admit.

When we play the last song of the night, my eyes flick up to find Ford, of all people, standing on the VIP balcony. I didn't know he was going to be here tonight, but it sends tension rippling through me. Until I see him give me a distinct thumbs up.

Fuck.

Well, all right then.

That ends the set on a fucking fantastic note, and when we head backstage, even though it's almost one o'clock, I'm feeling wide awake, riding the natural high of performing for a crowd.

Nils, Alexsis, and Maxi appear as the roadies start breaking things down.

"Great show, West," Nils says, slapping me on the back. "Can't wait for the tour."

"You and me both, dude," I assure him.

He and Alexsis slip away and Maxi steps up.

"You can tell me you thought we were awesome," I tease her with a wink.

She huffs and crosses her arms. "You were okay."

I laugh. Damn, she's stubborn. "I saw you out there. You were having fun, Maxi Marshall."

"Fine," she admits. "I might have enjoyed it … a little."

"Have it your way," I reply. A sudden thought sends a pang shooting through my chest. "Maxi?"

"What, West?"

"I'm going to miss you."

"I'm right here."

"No, when this is over, I mean."

Her eyes search my face. "But I'm so mean to you."

I smile at her. "I don't think you're mean. You just don't take my shit. I like that."

She rolls her eyes.

"And I like how much you roll your eyes at me."

Maxi scoffs. "You're so weird."

I chuckle. "Maybe. Or maybe I just need someone to keep me on my toes. To tell me the truth when I need to hear it."

"Are you trying to get in my pants or something?" she asks accusatorily.

Now I full-on laugh, holding my stomach and everything.

"It's not that funny," she murmurs after a minute.

I finally settle back down. "It is. Because there's

so much more to you than your pants, Maxi. So much more."

"Oh god, Alexsis was right."

I look at her curiously. "About what?"

"It's like boys on the playground. They tease you because they like you. You like me!" she gasps incredulously.

I cock an eyebrow. Hm. There's a thought. "And if I do?"

"You can't like me. You hate me!"

"I don't."

"Oh, you so do."

"I really don't."

"I don't believe you," she insists.

The problem is, she's not entirely wrong. When this all started, I didn't like her. And sometimes she still gets under my skin. But I respect her. And fuck it if she's not right. I think I like her. No, I know I like her. She's feisty and funny and caring. And gorgeous. Especially right now, looking like the goddess queen of groupies, even aside from her outfit. Her eyes are lit up, her energy hypnotic. She's every rock star's wet dream.

"Shall I prove it?"

Before she can protest, I take a step to close the gap between us and lean in, lightly placing my lips to hers. I give her a second to stop me, but when she doesn't, I lift my hand to her face, slipping it behind her neck, and threading my fingers through her silky hair to hold her in place while I really kiss her.

It takes a minute, but she starts to respond, her lips working against mine. And like a trigger's been pulled, my whole body responds, molding against her, my other arm slipping behind her to pull her even closer. I swipe my tongue into her mouth and she groans. The sound wakes my whole body in a way it hasn't been in far too long. And then we're all lips and heat and gasping for breath … that is, until I let her go.

She stares up at me, panting and confused.

"We may drive each other crazy," I murmur. "But I kind of dig it. Tell me you dig it too, Maxi."

"I do," she admits softly. Then her brows bunch together and she whispers, "Fuck."

That gets another laugh out of me. "Know what day it is?" I ask her.

"Tax day?" she snarks.

"Well, technically that was yesterday. Which makes today —"

"April sixteenth. Crap, West, it's your goddamn birthday."

My eyebrows shoot up. "You know when my birthday is?"

She levels a look at me. "I was your biggest fan

for a long time, remember? Of course I know when your birthday is." She holds up a hand at the look on my face. "And before you get any ideas, there will be no sexual birthday presents just because I had a mental lapse and let you kiss me."

"You kissed me back," I protest.

She purses her lips. "Okay, I kissed you back."

"I wasn't going to ask for sex."

"I said sexual."

"Well, I wouldn't say no to a blow job," I tease.

And she *punches* me. Though I kind of deserved it.

"Ouch," I say, feigning injury as I rub my arm. "I was kidding."

"No, you weren't."

"Okay, I wasn't. But really, this is weird for me too. I didn't plan to kiss you."

"Then why did you?" she asks, her eyes going soft.

I step into her, reaching up to palm her cheek. I try to find an explanation, but I don't fully understand it myself.

"I don't know," I admit. "When we first met, I thought I couldn't stand you. But something changed. And now … maybe I can't stand to be without you."

She closes her eyes and sighs. I lean down and kiss her again, this time going slowly. I realize something about holding her just feels right. Like all the other bullshit just goes away. In a way, it's a little like being high. Mind-numbing, but in a good way.

This is why they warn you against relationships right when you get out of rehab. Thankfully, rehab was a long time ago.

Because as I taste her, as her tongue meets mine and every neuron in my brain says "more," well, I'm pretty sure Maxi Marshall is my new drug of choice.

15

Sharp Dressed Man by ZZ Top

Max

"And you haven't seen him since after the private concert?" Alexsis asks, stunned.

"Nope."

"Wow," she mouths. "He didn't even call?"

"Oh, he did."

"And you didn't answer," she surmises.

"No."

"And … why not? You admitted you like him. What's your hang-up?"

I take a deep breath. "I do like him. More than like him. That's what scares me."

"You think he's going to break your heart again," she offers.

"Bingo."

"Always a risk," she agrees.

I give her a look. "Thanks. That makes me feel so much better," I tell her sarcastically.

She chuckles. "Well, if it helps, you look like a million bucks," she offers.

I look down at my pale pink lace and tulle gown, my brown waves sleeked over one shoulder. And I know my makeup is subtle but on point.

"I do, don't I?" I reply airily. "You look pretty fantastic yourself."

She twirls in her silver sequined mermaid dress. "Why, thank you."

"Any chance you invited a certain club manager to attend the airing party tonight?" I ask.

"Nils? Why would I invite him?" she asks, confused.

I laugh. "Oh, Alexsis. My dear, sweet, Alexsis. You like him, right?"

She blushes bright pink. "He's way too old for me."

"He's what, thirty?"

"Thirty-four."

"That's only twelve years," I say, though admittedly that's no small deal. "Besides, he obviously likes you too."

She brushes me away. "Oh, he does not."

"Mhm," I murmur. "Whatever you say." Then I mouth "he totally does" and she bursts out laughing.

"Whatever. Is our ride here yet or what?"

I check the app on my phone. "Just about. We can probably head out."

We catch our ride and head to the theater where the airing party is being held. We're arriving early, so I'm not particularly self-conscious about our ride. A limo would just be too weird for me.

I have to admit, I'm extremely curious to watch the fully edited show. Though seeing myself on screen will be a trip. Why does everyone always hate their own voice? Being a journalist, I should probably get over that.

In any case, we head in and meet Carter, Ford, and Burke. Jason, our boss, was going to come too but got sick. So we're left to hold our own. Thankfully, it's literally just the viewing plus an optional after-party.

Apparently, Ford and Burke have seen the finished product, but the tour sponsors will be watching it right alongside the public, so they'll see the reaction play out on social media in real time. All of the lead-up posts had great responses, though, so I'm not too worried.

But if I were West, I probably would be.

Speaking of West, I'm obviously nervously waiting for him to arrive. While trying to pretend I don't care at all. Fooling absolutely nobody, not even myself.

I guess I shouldn't be surprised when the lights blink, signaling that showtime is imminent, and he still hasn't appeared. That's a rock star for you. They arrive when they're damn good and ready.

The show starts, and it's just as jarring watching myself as I thought it would be. But West … goddamn he looks good on camera. None of his magnetism is lost.

The band interview plays well, coming across as funnier than I remember it being. But then, I was so nervous. And irritated.

Erik's apology is interesting to watch, since I wasn't close enough to hear everything while they were bowling. It's likewise equally funny and touching. Still light.

Then comes the ex. Dear god. It's even crazier on screen, with close-up camera work on Sadie's surprise freak-out attack. The audience gasps and oohs appropriately, lapping it up.

Annika's segment, however, brings the mood down considerably, but with just enough tenderness, particularly in West's very emotional post interview, it's bound to melt hearts across the world.

But the second it transitions to the apology with his father, I realize I can't watch this part. I don't want to watch this part. Alexsis's mouth pops open as I quietly and quickly bustle out of the theater.

As soon as I've closed the door behind me, the anxiety about that encounter begins to mellow.

"Well, that took you longer than I expected."

I whirl around at West's voice to find him standing in the foyer. In a black-on-black-on-black three piece suit and tie that's perfectly tailored to his slim, fit frame, he's more handsome than he has any right to be.

"What?" I ask blankly.

He chuckles, walking slowly toward me with his hands in his pockets.

"I guessed that you wouldn't last fifteen minutes. So kudos to you for lasting almost a whole hour."

He stops right in front of me. The smell of his expensive cologne fills my senses.

"You didn't go in at all, did you?" I ask, trying to ignore how close he is.

He shakes his head. "I lived it. That was enough."

I nod, unsure of what to say in response. His eyes rake over my lips, and I have to stop myself from shivering.

"You never called me back," he eventually points out.

"I'm sorry," I reply honestly. "This has all just been really overwhelming."

He laughs, and there's that smile. His real one. Not the snarky one. Not the teasing one. The genuine one. My favorite one.

"I have an idea what that's like," he replies. He tips his head toward double doors on the opposite side of the foyer. "I'm pretty sure they've already got the appetizers out in there. Hungry?" He offers a hand.

I reach out and take it. "Starved."

He leads me across the intricately patterned carpet at a leisurely pace. "By the way, you look absolutely stunning," he says casually.

"Thanks. You look pretty sharp in that suit."

"Aw, this old thing?" he replies with a wink.

He leads me through the double doors and into the after-party space. Against the wall to our right is a long banquet table that is, in fact, laden with appetizers and flutes of sparkling champagne. All ready for a celebration.

As I load up a plate, I can't help chuckling to myself.

"What?" West asks.

"I just think it's funny that you showed up late to

the airing that you didn't even end up watching, but you're early for the party. That sounds about right."

He smirks at me. "Hardy-har. West likes to party."

"Oh no, I didn't mean it like that," I say, giving him a concerned look.

He smiles and pops a mini quiche in his mouth. "I know. Champagne?"

I wave it away.

"You don't have to abstain just because I'm not drinking," he says with a frown.

"Oh, that's not why. It just feels premature to celebrate."

He raises an eyebrow. "Worried for me, are you?"

I pop a grape in my mouth. "Of course. Aren't you?"

The door bursts open before he can respond and Alexsis runs in, brandishing her phone. "There you are," she exclaims, stopping in front of us and thrusting the phone under West's nose. "You're a trending hashtag." She beams, pointing.

And sure enough, her social media tracker has #forgiveWest trending high on all major social media platforms. With exponential increase over the last hour that's continuing.

"Uh, I don't speak social media," West says. "Someone care to explain?"

Burke saunters up just as others begin to file into

the room, the rest of the band foremost. "It means you just saved all your asses," Burke explains. "Actually, mine too, come to think of it." He claps West on the back. "Good job, kid."

"Seriously?" West asks, jaw dropping. "The tour is on?"

Burke tips his head side to side. "Well, that'll officially be up to the sponsors. But I think it's pretty safe to say … yes. The tour is on. And our contact at the label texted me the thumbs up."

Everyone whoops and hollers. And now it feels like a celebration. Champagne is handed out, save West, who gets cider, and everyone cheers and toasts to West's victory. To not only saving the tour and contract, but to bringing the band back to relevancy, if the continued social media trend throughout the night is any indicator.

Well, at least for as long as they can ride this momentum. And with the tour promo ramping up, I have no doubt they will.

After about an hour of celebrating and networking, I'm a little peopled out. I try to say goodbye to West, but he's absolutely surrounded and grinning like he just won the lottery. So instead I say goodbye to Alexsis, who is also clearly enjoying herself, and head out to get a ride home.

I'VE ONLY BEEN HOME LONG ENOUGH TO TRADE THE beautiful but uncomfortable gown for sweats and a T-shirt when there's a knock on the door.

A quick glance out the peephole drops my jaw. I swing the door open.

"Why aren't you at your party?" I demand.

West smirks at me. "I had more important places to be."

I step back in shock, letting him in. "West, you just got your goddamn career back. My apartment cannot possibly be the most important place right now."

I close the door behind him and stare at him, hands on hips.

He steps into my space, reaching up to hold my chin.

"See, now, that's where you'd be wrong. Sure, it felt good to know that I did it. That the tour is on. That everything is going to be okay. But when I realized you were gone … I felt like I was missing something. Because without you, none of this would've been possible. So it would seem that wherever you are … well, that's the most important place."

I pull his hand down. "Don't say things like that."

"Why not? It's true."

"Maybe. But you can't just say things like that."

"Things like what?"

"Things that make me feel for you," I shout. So loud that I clap my hand over my mouth. "I'm sorry."

He chuckles and steps back into my space. "You're not alone, Maxi. I feel it too. Even when you yell." He lifts his hand and strokes it down my cheek, and it chips at the wall around my heart. "And I feel it when I touch you." He leans in, grazing his lips ever-so-softly against mine. The wall cracks. "And I definitely feel it when I kiss you."

His mouth presses harder into mine, and the wall comes tumbling down. I wrap my arms around his neck just as he pulls me into him. Our mouths quickly become hungry, tongues tangling, lips taking, as my hands wind into his thick, dark hair and he pulls me by my ass against him. I can feel his arousal between us and I groan, twisting my hips with need.

His head drops to my neck, licking and sucking at the sensitive spot just under my ear.

"I need you, Maxi," he says huskily into my ear.

I sigh happily. Because as much as I've fought it, I think I need him too.

"Are we really doing this?" I ask, dazed.

West pulls back, bringing things to a screeching halt. My body hums for him to keep doing what he'd been doing, but my brain is glad for the breather.

"Obviously I want to." His hand cups the back of my neck. "But we're only doing this if it's what you want too."

Laughter bubbles out of me. "I've wanted this since I was seventeen years old," I admit.

His brows shoot up. "Damn, you sure know how to make a guy feel special."

I grab him by the lapels of his suit jacket, marveling at the silkiness of the expensive material. "You are special, West. More than I think you know. More than even I knew."

I stare up into his eyes. And even if he doesn't fully appreciate the truth in those words, in this moment, I do. West has remade himself. He's done everything asked of him and more to reclaim what he'd lost, at no small cost.

And though I was deeply disappointed in him for a time, he's shown me that he's not the person that addiction made him into anymore. The enigmatic, talented, and impassioned musician I fell for from afar has returned in the form of this man whom I've come to respect and admire, despite our preferred method of communication being sass. Or maybe a little bit because of it.

When he doesn't respond to my assertion, I decide I don't need him to. I'm ready to stop holding back. To take a chance on West. He's earned it. And it's time for me to stop lying to myself about how I really feel.

"Touch me, West," I beg.

"Fuck, Maxi," he breathes. "Anything for you."

His fingers skate down my neck, to the collar of my shirt. His fingertips lightly feather over my breast as his hand comes to rest at my waist, slipping under the back of my shirt.

His warm hand slides up my back, pinching the clasp of my bra until it pops open. He grins down at me.

"Time to take this off," he commands.

I bite into my bottom lip, gripping the hem of my shirt. And I slowly start walking backward, leading him to my bedroom. Unsurprisingly, he follows.

Once we're inside, I raise the hem of the shirt inch by inch, finally slipping it over my head. I shimmy my bra off and let it fall to the floor with the shirt. I put my hands on my hips.

"Your turn," I tell him.

West just stands in the doorway, hands in his pockets, staring at my chest. His eyes are dark, his body uncannily still.

"West?" I prompt.

"I'm sorry, I just … look at you, Maxi. Wow."

"Oh, you haven't seen anything yet," I promise with a sultry smile.

I hook my thumbs in my sweats, inching them down. He licks his lips. So I inch them down farther. His hands pop out of his pockets, opening and closing. I let the sweats fall to the floor with my panties before stepping out of them. He stands there, staring for a moment longer before taking three long, purposeful strides and stopping in front of me.

I look up at him. His eyes are practically obsidian and he's radiating heat. A shiver runs down the length of my body. And he hasn't even touched me yet.

Instead, he uses his body to walk me backward until I hit the bed. Then in one swift move he lifts my legs and has me on my back. I cry out in surprise, but I'm abruptly interrupted by his mouth connecting with my core, causing me to cry out for other reasons.

Still, he uses only his mouth, his tongue tasting every inch between my legs. Swirling over my most sensitive spot. Dipping into me teasingly. Setting a mad pace between the two.

He pulls away. "Maxi, look at me."

I lift my head and our eyes meet. His eyes don't leave mine as he slides two fingers into me. As he begins to pump them. As he reaches up with his other hand to apply pressure to my clit just so …

And I'm coming. I throw my head back as my orgasm explodes through my center, the energy spreading quickly through my entire body. I hit my peak and let out a sigh, cresting back down languidly as he withdraws.

As he pulls off his tie and shucks the rest of his clothing, I scoot back to the head of the bed and watch. I've seen pictures of West with his shirt off before, but I've never seen it in person. So when he removes the jacket, vest, and shirt, I'm treated to a pleasant surprise. He's more cut than he ever was in his younger years, though not bulky. His biceps, though … I didn't realize how huge they were. I'm definitely staring at him as hard as he was at me.

"Careful or you might set me on fire with that look," he says with a teasing note in his voice.

My eyes flick up to meet his. "I'm not sorry. You're fucking hot, West."

He laughs and crawls over the bed to me, capturing my lips with his. I pull at his unlatched belt, freeing it from his pants. As I work at the button on his slacks, he pulls back.

"I'm going to say this now, because I'm pretty sure once you get these off I'm not going to be up for talking," he teases.

I raise an eyebrow. "Oh?" I don't admit how much the implied promise makes my toes curl.

He smirks down at me, balancing over me in a way that makes his biceps that much more defined. God, I just want to lick them.

"I haven't had sex with anyone in over two years," he admits. "And STDs were, thankfully, one of the few things I managed to avoid. You?"

I pull a surprised face that he doesn't miss but also doesn't comment on.

"It's been a year. And I'm clean," I reply.

He grins. "Good." He leans in and kisses me chastely. "Are you on birth control?"

"Yep. Shots. But I'd still prefer to use condoms. You okay with that?"

West leans in, running his nose down my neck. "I just basically heard you say you're ready for me to fuck you," he murmurs in my ear. "So I don't care if you want me to wear a fruit roll-up, there's no way I'm saying no."

I laugh and lean toward the nightstand, fishing out the box of condoms that's probably gotten dusty, it's been in there so long. I check the date, hoping that they aren't expired.

"Oh thank god, there's a good month left on these," I say with relief.

"Are you sure? Because I can always go get more," he teases, pretending like he's about to leave.

"Just get over here and fuck me," I reply impatiently.

He grins and climbs onto the bed. "Yes, ma'am."

And as promised, he stops talking and removes his pants in earnest.

When he turns back to me, I get a full view of exactly how ready he is for this. But after more than two years, that's not exactly surprising. Still. The sight of him hard for me is just … mind-blowing.

He reaches over me to grab a condom while I'm busy staring at his cock, then lets me keep watching as he rolls it down his length.

As he settles between my legs, I continue to watch him in disbelief. He stares down at where our bodies meet, carefully rubbing himself over me. I throw my head back. It feels so damn good. And as he presses at my entrance, easing himself in slowly, I almost lose it.

"God, Maxi, you're so tight," he says.

And then he moves and holy shit.

I gasp and open my eyes to find him watching me. I bite into my bottom lip and he goes harder. I nod and he tips his head back, clearly enjoying this as much as I am as he goes even faster.

Watching him fuck me is the sexiest thing I have ever or will ever see. The tight muscles of his stomach contract, his dark eyes are hooded, the low rumbling in his chest beyond turning me on.

I move with him, encouraging him to keep building. And as he does, the beginnings of an orgasm start to swirl in me again.

"Maxi."

My eyes pop open, though I hadn't realized they were closed. His dark eyes meet mine, and I can see in their depths why he brought me back. He's close to the edge.

I pull him down to meet me, kissing him sweetly before wrapping my legs around him. I tilt with him, hard and purposefully, and moments later he's groaning out his orgasm, his face buried in my hair. My orgasm sputters, hanging in the balance as he slows.

I whimper, and his head snaps up, his eyes meeting mine. I see the realization there.

And he picks up the pace again.

"Oh," I exclaim, surprised at how hard he still is.

"You like that?" he murmurs in my ear, pumping again.

"Yes," I admit on a groan.

He keeps going, somehow still hard. The tightening in my low belly intensifies, my orgasm regaining speed. Knowing he can't do this forever, I slip my hand between us, swirling a finger over my clit in time to his thrusts.

He leans up on his arms and watches me as he continues to fuck me. I nod my encouragement. He goes harder. My free hand grips the pillow behind my head and I wordlessly nod, swirling faster.

He starts slamming so hard it hurts, but it's exactly what I needed to tip me over the edge. My back bows against the force of the climax that unfurls in my veins. His hand reaches down to grip my hip, joining us as deeply as he can, and it sends pleasure ricocheting through my entire body once more.

As I relax, I slump back down. I feel totally boneless as I stare up at him. He's sweaty and panting and a complete surprise. What kind of man comes then keeps going just to get you off?

I shake my head in disbelief. And gratitude. God, that was hot.

And then another thought flits through my mind. I just got thoroughly fucked by Kristoffer Westberg. I bite my lip, but it doesn't stop the shit-eating grin that spreads over my face.

"Well, you look happy," he remarks as he pulls out and makes to dispose of the condom.

"After that? How could I not be?" I murmur happily.

He slides back into bed next to me. "Good," he says, placing a kiss on my neck. "Because after we've rested, we are going to do that again."

"Promise?" I ask with another grin.

God, I can't stop smiling. It was beyond good. And the thought of doing it again … well, I don't dare to hope he enjoyed it as much as I did. Because giving in and believing he really wants me are two different things.

He rolls on top of me, caging me under him. I slide my arms around his neck. "Promise. I'm just sad we waited so long to figure this out."

"Figure what out?" I ask, puzzled.

"How good we are together."

I worry at my bottom lip. He can't mean what my heart wants to hope he means. No. He surely must mean all the bickering we've done could've been avoided if we'd simply just hopped in the sack together in the first place.

"Cute. But I don't think sex would've magically fixed all of our problems."

West grins and leans in, kissing me gently. "I'm not just talking about sex."

My heart melts. And with those six words, I'm a goner.

16

Bad Case of Loving You by Robert Palmer

West

As I enter band rehearsal on Monday, I'm greeted by a slow clap. And it's not just the band. There's actual crew today, which means tour prep has officially begun.

I grin like a fool, spreading just one arm out since I'm carrying Rosie with the other, welcoming the attention. The recognition that I pulled it off, from the people who really count. It probably doesn't hurt that I just spent the last two days buried in Maxi either, which was its own kind of reward. Yep. Right now, life is pretty fucking good.

"Thank you, thank you," I call magnanimously. "You may all bow and scrape now."

Nik approaches and punches me playfully in the gut. "You wish," she taunts.

I double over, feigning injury. "Not the thanks I was hoping for."

She smirks and picks up her bass, hopping up onto the small stage.

James walks by and claps me on the back. "Punching is Nik-speak for 'I'm proud of you,'" he jokes.

I shoot him a smirk knowing that's James-speak for "I'm proud of you too." But nothing is less rock and roll than hugging and sharing your emotions. So I know that's the most I'm going to get from any of them. Except maybe Ward when we're alone. Dude's scarily in touch with his feelings these days.

With a chuckle, I unzip the gig bag and get Rosie ready for rehearsal. "Yeah, yeah," I grumble teasingly. "West took one for the team, whatever."

"Hey, we played our parts," Michael protests. "I mean, I can't say it wasn't fun hearing you grovel, though."

I snort. "Too bad it was all for the cameras then, huh?"

I'm looking down as I tune Rosie, but when eerie silence falls after my words, I look back up.

Everyone is staring at me.

"What?" I ask innocently.

"Are you fucking kidding me?" Ward pipes up.

My head swings toward him standing at the mixing boards with one of the techs.

"Uh. No. You all knew it was just for show." A bunch of shocked faces stare back at me and my heart drops. "You didn't know?"

"Uh. No," James mocks. "Seriously, West?"

I set Rosie down carefully, because I just went from zero to pissed in two seconds flat, and I don't want to hurt her. "Seriously. I signed up to do what was asked of me. Nobody ever said it had to be real."

"That was kind of the whole fucking point, though, wasn't it?" Nik says. "I mean, why even do it if you didn't mean it?" She shakes her head in disgust.

"You guys can't be serious," I insist. I gesture at Nik. "You're the one who said, 'Just go with it.'" Then I fling an arm Michael's direction. "And you were the one who told me if I didn't do it, we were done. So I fucking did what I had to. Nobody ever said it had to be real."

"And I said not to be selfish," James points out. "That you weren't done making this up to people."

"I *humiliated* myself on a worldwide broadcast seen by hundreds of millions of people," I seethe. "A broadcast, that I might add, once it was edited and narrated bore little resemblance to what actually happened anyway. It was all a PR opportunity mashed up with placating the masses. Even if there had been any truth in there, it would've been lost in editing."

Ward shakes his head as the techs skitter out the door, clearly realizing this shit isn't going to get better and not wanting to get caught in the middle.

"What about your own conscience, man?" Ward nudges.

"My demons are my own. The only people whose opinions I care about are in this room," I insist.

"Yeah, and what about us?" Ward presses, now the clear voice for the group as everyone else has fallen silent. "Was your apology to us bullshit too?"

I press my lips together, and if looks could kill, Ward would be six feet under.

"Don't go there." I shoot glares at each of them. "Look, you guys may be pissed off at me, but I really thought you knew. Either way, this absolutely does not leave this fucking room unless you want to undo everything I worked for. Because whether the apologies themselves were real or not, I just went through a whole ration of shit to get us back on track. I swear I thought I was doing what you guys wanted me to. So please, don't throw me under the bus now. You'd just be fucking yourselves over."

Nik snorts. "We're not stupid. Of course we're not

going to say anything."

James stares at me sadly. Then, after a minute offers, "I'll talk to the techs too."

My gaze flips back to Ward.

"All right. What about Max, then, West? Don't think I don't know where you slipped off to on Friday night. Where you've been all weekend."

"Oh, so you're stalking me now, are you?" I throw at him accusingly.

Ward shakes his head. "I'm just looking out for you, bro. Things have clearly changed between you two. How's Max going to feel when she finds out?"

"She's not in this room, is she?" I snap back.

By his expression I can tell he gets exactly what I mean. I hadn't planned on telling her, even though I'm pretty sure she already knows.

But then, I thought the band knew too.

And clearly Nik gets my meaning too, because she can't keep herself from jumping in and offering, "This is the chick who hated you? You're with her now?" She snorts. "Yeah. Lying to her seems like a great idea."

"What is this, thank-West-by-making-him-feel-like-shit day?" I snap. But deep down I'm irritated because I know they have a point. About Max, at least.

If she doesn't already know like I thought she did,

how will she take it? Will she be furious? Or will she understand that I was doing what I had to?

"No," Michael mutters, going back to adjusting his kit. "Apparently this is bitch-smack-West-with-reality day."

"Great. Consider me bitch-smacked," I reply sarcastically. "Can we just rehearse already?"

Michael shrugs noncommittally. Everyone else stays silent but goes back to setting up, except for James, who I can only assume is going to talk to the techs before bringing them back in.

Great. Just fucking great. A few minutes ago I was high on life. And now I'm debating whether I should play it safe and keep my mouth shut or risk it all so see if I've started something with Max on a foundation of lies.

As I finish tuning Rosie, I let out a heavy sigh. Because I know what I have to do. It's what I should do. It's what the me of a few years ago would've never done. I've got to talk to her.

God, I hope I was right in the first place. I hope she already knows.

But my decision just proves how bad I've got it for Maxi Marshall. Because the last thing I want to do is break her heart by lying. But to be the guy she deserves, if I'm wrong, I may end up breaking her heart with the truth.

17

You Give Love a Bad Name by Bon Jovi

Max

What's the best way to cap off one of the best weeks of your career as a rock music journalist? Sex. Definitely sex. With a rock star. Which I'm very much looking forward to when West gets here … oh, any minute now.

I imagine most people would want to go slow. I mean, we just got together a week ago. Or maybe have dinner first. And sure, I'm hungry. But all week, I was sent messages about the show. Fans wanting to know if we're going to share more content online. Band managers asking me to feature their acts. The owners of the magazine personally gushing about what a great job I did.

Sure, I'm proud of myself. But every bit of praise made me think of West. How none of it would've been possible without his stubborn ass tracking me down. And how far he's come since then. How far *we've* come.

It didn't hurt that he spent most of last weekend showing me all the ways he knew how to use those talented fingers of his. Plus, you know, the rest of him.

And the pillow talk. Good lord. I forgot what the beginning felt like. Fresh and exciting and … well, pretty much a lust fest.

And I'm ready for Lust Fest Part Deux.

Dressed in skintight black jeans and a low-cut Sex Pistols tee, I definitely look groupie-level hot. So I'm pretty confident he's not going to care about skipping straight to the good stuff.

He's only fifteen minutes late when there's a knock on the door. I'd call that progress.

I swing the door open with a grin, ready for seduction … only to find, in place of the smoking hot sex god musician, there's a broody tired-as-fuck-looking hot mess of a man leaning against my doorframe.

"West?" I say, bemused.

His eyes search mine. All of the warmth and playfulness they usually hold is absent. A pit forms in my stomach.

"Can I come in?" he finally says.

I step back. "Sure, of course."

As I close the door, he walks in, kicking off his shoes and settling onto my old, tan leather couch. Well, sitting. He's not particularly settled as I take a seat next to him. More like perched on the edge of the cushion. And one finger is drawing circles on his knee. Shit.

"Rough week?" I ask tentatively.

His eyes flick up to meet mine.

"I have to ask you a difficult question," he hedges.

Something about his tone makes the pit in my stomach grow. "Okay," I reply slowly.

He looks down and his finger continues to work clockwise on his dark jeans.

"The apology tour," he starts. "Did you ..." He looks up at me "...did you believe it?"

My brows scrunch together.

"Are you worried that it seemed fake?" I ask.

He shakes his head. "No. I know the public ate it up. I'm asking if *you* believed it."

I lean back, unsure quite how to answer that. "Um. Yeah? I guess. I mean, you probably remember that I gave you shit at the beginning because your apology with Ward seemed too easy. And, you know, we both know the one with your dad was fake as fuck. That's not to say I blame you in the least. But other than that … of course." I pause, trying to work out what's bothering him. "Did someone else call bullshit? Is that what's upsetting you? Because I'll totally kick their ass."

He huffs a small laugh at the joke. "So if the other apologies *were* fake … would you blame me?"

I open my mouth to respond as the words sink in. And then I close it. Is he saying what I think he is? Part of me wants time to think about this before I speak, but unfortunately my brain-to-mouth filter just isn't that good.

"Were they?" I ask bluntly as I feel heat creeping up the back of my neck. A dangerous mix of anger and embarrassment churns under my skin, making me feel itchy all over.

West closes his eyes and sighs. "Yes."

And suddenly I want to vomit.

I was right. My first instinct was right and he …

"You *lied* to me." The irate words tumble from my mouth.

West opens his eyes and looks at me. His gaze is full of sorrow, regret, and exhaustion.

"Not on purpose. It may sound ridiculous, but I thought you knew."

I bark a sharp laugh. "You're right, that is ridiculous. I explicitly said I didn't want to participate if it was all for show. If it was all bullshit and didn't mean anything to you. Why even bother if it didn't?"

I rise as I speak, pacing in front of the couch.

"That's pretty much what Nik said," he mumbles. Then he catches my hand, forcing me to turn toward him. "I'm sorry, Maxi."

It takes all of my strength not to scoff at his apology. Because I can see that he's sorry, and I know firsthand how difficult it is for him to apologize. But sometimes sorry just isn't enough.

"You're *sorry*," I say sarcastically. "Well, that just fixes everything." I glare at him. "Your sister? Was that a lie?"

West shoots up in front of me. "God, no," he protests, grabbing my other hand and holding both in his. "At least, not all of it. I really did apologize to her."

I grind my teeth as I consider that. "Your band?"

West looks at me warily but doesn't respond. So yeah. That one was a lie.

"Holy shit, West. Your brother? Sadie?"

He nods. Both lies.

"Me? Your apology about the night at the Forum? The one just now? Are those lies too?" I ask, my voice strained with emotion.

"Absolutely not," he responds vehemently. "How could you even think that?"

My eyebrows fly up. How could I think that? Is he joking?

"Because now I have no idea what's truth and what's a lie. Why should I believe you? You could be lying that you weren't lying."

West pulls a face. "What?"

I wave my hands in frustration. "I can't do this. You should go."

"Wait, Maxi, please, I —"

"No, West. No. Whatever you're going to ask. No. I can't. I already gave you another chance and you blew it. But even if you hadn't already screwed me over once, I can't trust someone who lies to me. And I can't be with someone I don't trust."

West's face caves and despite myself, it hits me right in the gut. I want to reach out and comfort him, but how do you comfort someone who has deceived you after having been forgiven for something even worse?

"Come on, Maxi, there has to be a way through this. Please," he begs.

He reaches his hand toward my face, but I take a step back. Knowing if he touches me I'll be that much more likely to give in.

I shake my head. "Maybe. But not right now.

Right now I need some time to process the truth. I think you should leave," I reiterate.

West goes to reach for me again but stops himself, his hand clenching into a fist and dropping to his side. "I'd rather stay and talk."

"Why? What else could you possibly have to say to me that would make any difference? What could be more important than the fact that you —"

"Because I love you," he all but shouts over me. Whatever words I had die on my lips at his confession. "I love you." His tone is softer and his eyes search mine softly. "I know, it doesn't make any sense. But I do. Please. Don't shut me out."

I blink hard against the tears. He means it. I can see that. Or at least, he thinks he does. But how could he possibly love me?

"You don't lie to someone you truly love, West. If you really want to be with me, you should go figure your shit out. For real this time," I persist.

"I thought I had," he says, sorrow dripping from every word. "But maybe I don't even know what that looks like."

"It looks like doing what's right when nobody else is looking. It looks like telling the truth when there's nobody who cares whether you're lying. But mostly, it's figuring out what's stopping you from doing those things."

"What happens if I never figure it out?" he challenges. "I just found you. I can't lose you now."

"You lost me before you ever knew what you had," I reply. "Because of your choices. And while I understand now more than ever how your choices have been shaped by … things out of your control … well, at the end of the day, they're your choices. And the consequences of them are also yours to deal with."

"So that's it?" he asks. And a tear skates down his cheek.

My heart cracks in half. Again.

But I don't let him see me cry. I simply nod.

"You can show yourself out," I say quietly.

And then I turn and head into my bedroom, closing the door behind me.

I put my back to the door, sliding to the floor. And then I let the tears go. Quietly, though, in case he lingers. But as soon as I hear the front door close, I don't hold back anymore.

If it's possible, this time hurts worse than the first. Or maybe it's the compounded betrayals. Or maybe it's because this time I wasn't the only one in love. This time it was real. Or at least, I thought it was.

18

King Nothing by Metallica

West

"Well, I hope you're happy," I grumble at Ward after everyone else has left rehearsal on the following Monday. A fucking shitty rehearsal, as it were. I was barely mentally present, focusing more on how pissed I am at all of their ungrateful asses.

Ward cocks an eyebrow at me. "Ah. Talking to me again, are you?" he asks dryly, plunking down on the couch by the door. The same one we used for the first apology interview. The irony isn't lost on me. "So what am I supposed to be happy about?"

I stay standing where I am at the equipment table.

"Max didn't know I was being less than truthful on the apology tour either," I grumble.

"Lying," Ward offers. "It's called lying, West. So how'd the truth go over?"

I look up and shoot him a glare. "About as well as you'd expect. She dumped me."

He nods slowly, the glint in his eye telling me he thinks I deserved it, but he doesn't say anything.

"Can I ask you a question?"

Ward smirks. "I have a feeling you're going to no matter what I say."

My nostrils flare. He's in full douchebag lead singer mode. His arms splayed over the back of the couch. One ankle resting on the other knee. His arrogance shining through that pretty face of his. One I'd love to punch right about now.

"If you thought my apology was honest, was your forgiveness?"

His response is automatic. "If the apology was bullshit, de facto so was the forgiveness. Whether I intended it to be or not." He pauses. "I think the better question is, why wouldn't the apology be real?"

His hard veneer slips a little and I can see the hurt behind the question. But if he thinks his wounded feelings compare to the reality of our history, he's got another thing coming.

"Oh, gee, I don't know, maybe because you're the one who got me into heroin in the first place?"

Ward snorts. I know he doesn't get it. He's not an addict. It's not how he's wired. Unless an addiction to being a know-it-all asshole is a thing.

"Yeah, and you got Annika addicted. You're no angel either, West."

"And I apologized," I point out. "The only apology that was real, might I add, because she's the only person who deserved an apology from me. The rest of you assholes did everything you could to encourage my behavior. You" — I jerk my chin at Ward — "so someone in the band was partying too. So it wasn't just you. Erik so he could feel superior in looking down his sanctimonious nose at me. Sadie because she needed the high from the drugs and from fucking a rock star. And my dad …" I trail off, shaking my head.

I can't say it. But I know it's because it made him feel secure that nobody would ever take me seriously. That I wasn't a threat to him because I couldn't keep my head straight long enough to function, much less bring to light everything he did.

"So why'd you pick us for your apologies then? Why do it at all, for that matter?"

"Because I had no other choice," I roar at him.

"But I'm sick of pretending I'm the only one who fucked up here."

Ward rises. "Look. I've tried to be supportive. I've tried to be patient. But the truth hurts, West. And the truth is, you're pointing your finger, but there's no one around to blame but you. Nobody forced you to take drugs. You could've said no. Nobody forced you to be a dick to Sadie, to abuse your little sister's trust, to be a complete asshole to your family. To your fans. To Max." He stops in front of me, his expression frustrated. "I'm glad you got clean, man. But if you're going to really get your life back, you need to start taking responsibility for your choices."

"You're a fucking hypocrite," I scoff, grabbing my gig bag and moving around him.

"Never said I was perfect," he calls to my back. "But at least I don't play the victim card."

And I've never seen red like I do in that moment. My brain disconnects from my body and I whirl, flying toward him, fist raising of its own accord.

The only mental clarity I have is noting the surprise on his face as I punch him.

— ♪ —

I WENT TO EXACTLY ONE NARCOTICS ANONYMOUS meeting before I decided they weren't for me, along with AA, sponsors, therapists, and everything else that I thought was for weak-ass pussies who couldn't keep their shit together.

Except, as I down my fourth double shot of Jack Daniels, I'm starting to think maybe it was less for pussies and more … well, to avoid exactly where I am right now. Thankfully, I'm already too drunk to care. Which is hilarious, because way back when, I'd just be getting started. And now I'm practically a light-weight. Well, by comparison. It's almost funny.

Or it would be if I wasn't still furious. At Ward. The band. Max. Myself. I'm also sober enough to know I should drag ass the few blocks home and sleep this shit off, rather than let it turn into what it would've back then too. Harder drugs. Preferably heroin, yes, but I'd never say no to cocaine either. And a good, high-as-a-kite fuck-fest, usually with Sadie and at least one of her stripper friends.

While I can't say I have easy access to those kinds of drugs anymore, it wouldn't be difficult either. And getting women … well, even before the apology tour, there were clearly enough of them who didn't care about my fall from grace and gladly would've fucked me. Not that I fucked any of them. Not since before rehab, anyway.

I was trying to be good. Trying to put my life back together and focus on the band. And until

Maxi, I didn't have the first clue how to be with someone while I was sober. Hell, I didn't have the desire to.

But I've lost her, just like I've lost Ward. And probably the rest of the band.

Boy, this tour is going to be fun.

I throw way too much money on the bar and stumble out onto the street.

The sun has just set, with the dimmest of deep pink and purple glows still visible over the darkening ocean waves across Pacific Coast Highway. It'd be beautiful if I wasn't in the middle of throwing myself a pity party.

Fucking ocean.

"Holy shit, guys, it's West!" I hear someone say behind me.

I realize as I look up that I'd been teetering on the edge of the sidewalk. I glance back at the group of dudebros behind me. There are three of them, and they look like a bunch of preppy-ass college punks looking to do some Jägerbombs, or whatever the kids are into these days.

One of them starts pulling out his phone as they rush at me. The one who I think spoke claps me on the shoulder.

"Dude, I can't believe it's you! You're awesome," he says.

One corner of my mouth tips up. Hey, at least the fans still love me. That's what I wanted … right?

"Thanks, man," I reply.

"Take a picture with us," the dudebro to his left says as the guy with the phone positions himself slightly in front of us with his camera front-facing to get us all in the shot.

I shrug. "Okay, sure, why not."

They get the picture, then dudebro number one, the one who spoke first, says, "Come drink with us."

I wave him off. "Nah, I gotta get home, man. Rehearsal tomorrow and everything."

Dudebro number two jumps in. "Come on. It's on us. Whatever you want man, just hang with us. Our friends would be so jealous if we bought you a drink."

And I'm just drunk enough that the appeal to my ego works. "Yeah, okay, just one drink," I agree.

I WAKE UP THE NEXT MORNING TO A CLANGING NOISE that sounds like a rhythmically challenged kid banging on a steel drum kit. What the fuck?

My surroundings start to come into focus. I'm on a hard surface. It smells bad. And as my blurry eyes adjust I realize … I'm in a motherfucking jail cell.

I bolt upright and my eyes land on a young police

officer leering at me through the bars, holding a night-stick up against the metal. That must have been what was causing the clanging.

"Rise and shine, pretty boy," he taunts. "Your manager is here to bail you out."

My head pounds and my stomach churns, and not just at the thought that I did something bad enough to land me here. Bad enough to need to be bailed out. But also because I'm pretty sure I drank the whole fucking bar last night.

At least, that's how it feels based on the level of hungover I am right now and how little I remember of the evening. I check myself before rising, mentally noting that at least I didn't vomit or piss all over myself. So I've certainly had worse nights.

As I'm led into the main office, I catch sight of Burke's expression. And if I didn't know better, I'd say someone died. I only hope it's not about to be me.

19

Under the Bridge by Red Hot Chili Peppers

Max

I'm woken early Tuesday morning by my phone ringing shrilly from the nightstand. I grope for it sleepily, fumbling as I attempt to slide to answer. I barely register that it's Jason.

"This better be good," I say, half joking, half serious. Because I also notice it's not even six a.m. Even if he is technically my boss, it still annoys me.

"I woke you up." It's not a question.

"So early, yet so observant," I grumble, sitting up in bed and rubbing my eyes. "What's up, Jason?"

There's silence from his end for a few moments.

"Christ, I thought you'd already be up. That you'd already know."

"Know *what*?" I ask, annoyed.

An incoming text pings in my ear. "I just sent you the link. Get in here once you've watched it. We're going to have a full day on our hands," he replies cryptically.

"O…kay?" I respond. But he's already hung up. Great.

With a tired sigh, I kiss my last hour of sleep goodbye and click the link Jason sent.

A YouTube video pops up and loads. The time stamp is almost one a.m. this morning. The only object I can make out as it loads is a wood surface of some kind.

"Duuuuude, you're *West*," says some surfer-dude-sounding guy from behind the shaky cellphone camera. The view lifts to focus on West, flanked by two other guys who appear college-aged. And they're clearly in a bar, drinks in front of all of them. The wood surface was the table.

I suck in a sharp breath and my heart starts pounding. No. No, no, no.

"I'm Weeeeest," he slurs in response lifting a glass of amber-colored liquid and downing it. "Fuck yeah, man!"

Exactly what I feared. West has fallen spectacularly — and very publicly — off the wagon.

The guy to West's left downs his drink and cheers. The guy to West's right holds up his glass.

"This one's for you, West. You're my fucking *hero*, man! You took it on the fucking chin with that apology tour, bro." Then the kid downs his drink.

West starts laughing.

"Did I say something funny?" The guy on the right asks blankly.

"No. I just hate to burst your bubble," West says, giggling. "But it was all fake."

Well, shit. He's fallen off the wagon and spilled the beans. I suddenly get exactly what Jason meant. This is officially a complete and utter disaster.

The guy on the left bursts out laughing just as the guy on the right sets down his glass, looking in shock at West.

"No, no way, dude," he says. "Come on. Really?"

"Yup. It was all total bullshit. Sorry." He shrugs. "In my defense, they made me do it."

I want to cover my eyes. I want to stop watching the train wreck. But I can't seem to make myself turn it off.

The kid on the right continues to look devastated. "That's just … that's just wrong," he says, his cheeks reddening in apparent anger.

West shrugs, then looks over at the guy holding the camera for the first time. "Dude, no more pictures," he slurs.

"It's not a picture," the guy holding the camera says in a taunting tone. "It's a video."

West's face goes from annoyed to angry in two seconds flat. "I didn't say you could record me, dude. Turn that shit off. Delete it."

Camera guy laughs. "Hell no, man, this shit is gonna blow up. Posting in three, two —"

West lunges for the camera and the remaining few seconds of video are a blur of fists and glass and wood.

I watch it again. And again. And again. Every viewing nauseates me more.

When I can't handle any more, I check the view count. It's already in the hundreds of thousands in the five or so hours it's been up.

Holy. Shit.

I drop my phone and put my hands over my face. West, what the fuck have you done?

— 🎶 —

"WHAT DO WE KNOW?" I ASK AS SOON AS I MARCH into Jason's office just after seven.

He stops typing and closes his laptop, gesturing

for me to take a seat. As I do, he gets up and closes his door, then returns to his chair.

He folds his hands on his desk and gives me a serious look.

"They arrested West last night for assaulting the kid making the video. West's manager is bailing him out as we speak. That's all I know right now, but I expect a number of things to happen today."

I nod, feeling sick at his words, even though I'd assumed as much.

"Let me guess," I hazard. "The video will continue to go viral. They'll call off the tour. They'll hold press conferences disavowing all knowledge that West's apologies weren't truthful."

Jason nods grimly. "At the very least. They're trying to get it taken down, as it's technically evidence in an active police case," he replies. "But it's a video of a major rock star breaking his sobriety, assaulting someone, and admitting he duped his fans. Now that it's out there, it's going to be practically impossible to stop."

I close my eyes for a moment, trying not to think about what this will mean. Determined to keep it together, I open them again and look back at Jason, whose face is filled with concern. Despite not knowing of my brief lapse in judgment in the sleeping-with-West department, he clearly understands that this will be tough for me. Because, oh yeah, my career and the magazine's reputation are on the line too. Goddamn West.

"What do you need from me?" I ask.

"I've already got PR working on a press release to go out this afternoon. They're going to want your input. And start working on an article detailing our involvement in the apology project to make it clear that we were explicit in participating only under the condition that this was a genuine endeavor. We were assured it was, and thus we had no knowledge to the contrary. Use examples from the tour — the sister would be a good one — that show you truly believed him to be sincere." He hesitates, then looks at me warily. "You didn't know he was faking it, did you?"

My chest tightens with anxiety. Because even though West lied to me, fell off the wagon, and utterly destroyed everything we worked for … I can't find it in me to betray him. Even if he's betrayed himself.

"I had suspicions at first, which West denied. So no, while we were filming I was under the impression that he wasn't faking it," I reply truthfully.

Jason examines my face for a few moments. And I know he's not stupid. He can clearly read between the lines. But I know he's also smart enough to realize there's no point in pushing the issue.

So he lets me go, finally free to be alone with my

thoughts while I try to figure out how on earth I'm going to write this article.

I haven't gotten far when I receive word that the tour has officially been cancelled. And Violent Mood Swings has been dropped by their label. The band, save West, has scheduled a press conference for early this afternoon that, thankfully, Alexsis will cover while I try to gather my thoughts on all of this.

I spend the day trying to distill a dangerous mix of emotions and facts into something that can salvage the magazine's reputation. While I manage it adequately, it's not without constant flipping between revisiting my anger at West's charade of an apology tour and concern knowing how devastated he must be. Because now he's truly lost everything.

It's underscored when Alexsis returns from the band's press conference. She tells me that every single one of them more or less threw West under the bus by blaming him and only him for the lies. I suspect they think they're doing it for his own good, trying to help him learn the lesson I also want him to learn: that at some point he needs to stop half-assing it and really fix things. But I know he'll only see it as a betrayal, a loss. And it is both of those things.

But the loss of his band, his *friends*, the fans, the tour, his record contract … and I guess you can toss me on that list too. Oh god, and his family. Now that this is out there they'll know he was lying. It's so much all at once.

It's going to crush West. And he's already slipped, as evidenced by his drunken toppling of everything left that he held dear.

My deepest fear is that this is going to achieve the exact opposite of showing him how much harder he needs to try. I'm terrified that it's only going to send him spiraling farther down, back into the abyss he only just climbed out of. Possibly even deeper.

Despite everything he's done to me, I don't want that for him. And it's with that thought I realize that I'd never stopped having feelings for Kristoffer Westberg. Not through any of this. Not since the very beginning. Even the negative feelings were fueled by knowing I still cared.

As much as I hurt for West, I don't even consider contacting him. He needs to feel this pain. To live with the weight of it. Because there's a slim chance that I'm wrong, that it will be exactly the wakeup call he needs to get his life back together, for real this time.

At least, that's what I'm hoping for. And you know what they say: Hope dies last.

20

Hurt by Johnny Cash

West

One minute, I'm floating. The next, a sharp jab in the ribs snaps me out of a light, drug-induced sleep.

It takes me a while to come to. Minutes? Hours? Who knows. Time has lost all meaning. Everything has lost all meaning. A pressing need to take a piss forces me to wake up enough so I can stumble to the bathroom sooner rather than later.

But opening my eyes, I'm not where I thought I'd be. Thankfully, I'm not in a jail cell this time, but being in a bed I don't recognize isn't exactly great either.

I lift my head and peer through the dim early morning light to find Sadie passed out next to me, her elbow lodged in my side.

Fucking awesome. I check myself over only to find I'm still fully dressed, though that could mean I'd gotten dressed afterward with the intention of leaving and just passed out before I could. The odds of being in Sadie's bed and not having fucked her are pretty low, unfortunately. At least, if our history is anything to go by.

As I climb out of bed and find her bathroom, I try to bring back my memories from last night. But all I can remember is yesterday morning, waking up in jail. Everything after that is gone. The kind of gone alcohol alone can't account for.

Given my still-detached senses and general calmness, I'm going with heroin, and not a small amount of it. A sniff of my shirt as I use the bathroom tells me there was also plenty of booze. And Sadie's signature jasmine scent clings to me.

I know I'm sobering up though, because I start feeling disgusted with myself on every level. I have no doubt I crawled back into Sadie's good graces just by having drugs. It doesn't matter how pissed she is, if I've got what she wants, she always takes me back. That's probably why I went to her; I know what a doormat she is. And some habits are hard to break. Many habits, apparently.

I head back to the bedroom but hesitate on the threshold. Just the sight of her sleeping there throws me back. It's my life before rehab all over again.

Except worse.

I start to remember everything that preceded this little bender, and I turn around, headed for the living room. I can't lose it within earshot of that crazy bitch. So instead, I swipe my cellphone, a pack of smokes, and a lighter from the bedroom and head for the door, intending to smoke outside before going back to find the wallet and keys I was unable to locate right away.

But on the way past the dining room, I spot a glass door that leads to a small balcony. That'll do.

I slip out, the cool morning air waking me quickly. I light up a cigarette, something else I haven't done in years. Christ, I really am on a roll, aren't I?

Well, if I'm going to completely blow my second chance, might as well do it properly. I take a deep drag and practically groan in relief at how fast the nicotine buzz hits.

My phone vibrates in my pocket, distracting me. I pull it out and see a text from Ward, among other notifications.

Seriously? Drunk dialing me? After everything

you've lost in the last 24 hours because of drinking?
DO BETTER.

I swallow hard as tears spring to my eyes. As the memories of yesterday land. Of finding out I'd been arrested for assault. Also known as punching some kid who made a video of me admitting the whole apology tour was a sham. And then said video exploding, outing my lapse in sobriety and the calculated duping of my fans. Which unsurprisingly led to the tour being cancelled and losing our record contract.

As if that wasn't bad enough, my band then completely turned on me for absolutely no reason. They didn't even have anything to gain from pointing the finger solely at me; we'd already lost everything. No, they just couldn't pass up the opportunity to kick me while I was down.

As I process Ward's text, it suddenly occurs to me that he may not be the only one I drunk-dialed. My stomach drops as I scramble to go through my calls and missed notifications.

Yep. I called Maxi. And she texted me back. Fuck fuck fuck fuck fuck.

I open her text and my breath leaves me.

If you care about me at all, you'll leave me alone and focus on yourself. Figure out what forgiveness really means and then maybe you can stop faking it. All of it.

I stare down at the phone, heart ripped in two. Wet spots appear on the glass and I realize I'm crying.

I've lost the band. I've lost my oldest friends in the world. I've lost Maxi. My family has probably seen the video. I couldn't give two fucks about my brother and father, but god, if Annika sees it … I close my eyes and fat tears slip under my lids and down my cheeks.

My world has been burned to the ground. And here I stand on the balcony of the succubus bitch who rode me for fame and drugs. Who would gladly continue to suck the life out of me.

I sink onto the concrete base of the balcony, pressing my head against the metal bars.

Figure out what forgiveness really means.

That's what Maxi said. But that's the rub — I have no idea what forgiveness means. I am sure of one thing though: This time I'm beyond forgiveness. I'm not going to get a third chance at this life.

I put out the cigarette butt and rise, leaning over the balcony. And if I thought I was crying before, it's nothing to the tears that fall stories and stories down to the pavement below.

Maybe I should just … lean farther. Let myself go. Stop fighting so fucking hard for a life that doesn't want me. The thought makes the tears fall faster, and a sob rips out of my chest. The metal rail cuts into my abdomen.

The pain snaps me out of it a little. That I can feel pain. That I'm alive. And knowing my fuck-up self, if I tried to jump, I probably wouldn't die. I'd probably end up paralyzed or in a coma or something, trapped in a body that no longer obeys me, just like my life doesn't.

For some reason the thought makes me laugh. I've really lost it now, and I should probably get my shit together and go home. At least fall apart in private. With a sad shake of my head, I go back inside.

21

Darkest Days by Stabbing Westward

West

"You better not have finished my smokes," Sadie greets me from the kitchen as I step back inside the dingy little apartment.

I roll my eyes and chuck the pack at her. "I only had one, keep your panties on," I grumble. My eyes scan the kitchen and dining room, not finding what I'm looking for. "Where's my wallet and keys?"

She laughs. "Oh don't worry, my panties were firmly on all night, no thanks to your limp dick," she shoots back venomously, then points toward the front door. "Your shit's on the floor over there."

Insanely relieved that I did not, in fact, fuck Sadie,

I stride over to the door and find my things exactly where she said, just inside on the floor. Clearly carelessly dropped there as we came in.

I snatch the items up and tuck them into my pockets.

"Well, it's been real," I call to her. "Have a nice life."

She snorts as she pours herself a cup of coffee. I mean, don't bother offering me any, bitch.

"Yeah, sure," she says dismissively. "Next time you come back, at least bring some vitamin V with you. It's a waste of heroin not to get a good fuck with it."

"I'm not coming back," I assure her. *And I'm definitely not touching you ever again*, I think to myself.

She leans against the counter, sipping her coffee. "If that's what you want to believe," she mutters.

"That's reality, Sadie. Last night was a huge mistake."

"So you're not going to get high again? Really?" she taunts.

I run a hand through my hair, agitated. I hadn't actually thought that far. Do I want to? Yes. And no. But she has a point — now that I've slipped, there's a very real chance I could slip again. And again. Until it's not slipping anymore. Until it's just my life.

Feelings stir in my chest. Fear. Guilt. Despair. And

I realize … I don't want that. This time I really, truly don't. Yesterday was … well, one of the worst days of my life. I was in a bad place. One I don't want to be in again.

"No," I reply resolutely. "I'm not."

She snorts. "Okay then. But when you do, we both know you're coming back for some ass," she says with a shrug, taking another drink.

I shake my head. "Don't you get tired of living like this, Sadie?"

"Don't you?" she shoots back caustically.

"I *am* sick of it. I fucked up last night."

She sets her mug down, coming around the counter between us and stopping in front of me.

"You did fuck up last night. But I know how you can make it up to me," she says sultrily, staring up at me from under her eyelashes.

I look down at her. Her makeup is smeared. And even though she's only twenty-six, the bags under her eyes, the sag of her skin from drugs, partying, and god knows what else, make her look twice her age.

With a feline grin, she presses against me, rubbing her hand over my cock.

A couple of years ago, I would've instantly grabbed her and fucked her up against the door. Now? Junior doesn't even stir. Not even a twitch. I'm well and truly repulsed by the situation.

How was I ever attracted to her? To this lifestyle?

I wasn't, is the answer.

So why did I let it consume me? That's the real question.

"Damn, West, there's something really wrong with you," she says, dropping her hand after getting no reaction. "I've fucked sixty-year-olds with harder dicks than yours."

I step back in disgust. This is all wrong. All of it.

"Well, then I'll leave you to go find a sixty-year-old to fuck," I tell her. "Bye, Sadie."

I walk out the door and down the stairs, stopping in front of her apartment building to text my driver for a ride home.

It doesn't take him long, and he doesn't ask questions. And I'm glad for it, because I already feel shitty enough.

As soon as I get home, I don't even shower. I head into my music room and grab my first guitar. I could have grabbed any of the dozen I own, but that one called to me.

As I settle onto my balcony, the late-morning May air finally starting to warm, everything still feels *wrong*. I know it shouldn't feel right, given how epically awful the last couple of days have been.

But this is the place I go so all of that can fade away. So I can let the music, the waves, the fresh air take it all away. Except it doesn't. I strum mindlessly, trying to find a song, any song, that will help me connect with what I'm feeling.

Problem is, I'm feeling way too damn much. Anger. Sadness. Defeat. Helplessness. No … I don't feel helpless, I decide after a few moments of turning the word over on my tongue.

I feel powerless.

I have no idea how to fix any of this. How to fix myself.

The last time I felt this wasn't before rehab. No, rehab was a court-ordered solution. It wasn't something I sought, though eventually it turned into something I chose to continue. No, the last time I was this low, I was sixteen and seemingly trapped in the hell that was my life. I was never smart like Erik. My music wasn't good enough for my pedophile father. Even I was almost too old for him to abuse anymore. But Annika … I can't even think of what he did to us. And when I'd try to use music to escape, he'd try to take that away too.

There was nothing right about my life. Everything felt wrong, *was* wrong. But I had no clue where to begin to make it right. Fuck, I was just a kid. What did I know about anything?

So I ran. Like a coward, though not before making Erik promise to take care of Annika. Since he was so adept at avoiding Dad, I thought he could help her. And I couldn't take it anymore. It was too heavy a burden to carry.

So I vanished and did my best to forget about it all. I lived on the streets for two years, playing my beat-up guitar for change and picking through garbage cans for food. Fighting with other runaways for territory. Stealing to survive. And when the opportunity presented itself, doing drugs to feel something besides the well of pain inside. In some ways it was better. But I never really forgot.

It wasn't until a month after my eighteenth birthday that I met Ward in front of a bulletin board outside of Guitar Center. And the rest, as they say, is history.

The tears start again at that thought. Because now it really *is* history. All of it. Because of me.

I know this has to stop. Because nothing has really changed since the darkest days of my life at age sixteen. I'm right back there now, at thirty-six.

Except now I'm not a helpless teenager with more scars and guilt than brains. And even if I don't know how to fix this any more than I did then, I know I can't keep burying those feelings. If I'm going to break this cycle, I need to dig them up and bring them into the light. Something I didn't even do in rehab.

I've avoided it, putting band-aids on the problem, hoping it'll just go away.

But the demons inside are clawing their way out. They're ruining my life. And clearly I'm not going to slay them on my own.

I need help.

The guitar slides from my lap. I lean forward, not fighting the tears for the first time. Letting them go.

Letting it all go.

22

Shout by Tears for Fears

West

Two months later…

"So. Kristoffer. How was your week?" Dr. Marks asks, tilting her head in that way only a therapist can.

"Well, Sherry," I tease her with a wink. "It wasn't bad, actually."

She smiles tolerantly, her amber eyes crinkling under her silver-rimmed glasses.

"Your energy does seem calm today," she remarks knowingly. "You went to your meetings?"

I nod slowly. "I'm down to one NA meeting a week," I respond.

"Still two AA meetings, then?" she asks, concern tinging her voice.

"Yep."

She makes a note, then looks back up at me. "I'm a little surprised. It's been two months. Do you still feel like you might relapse?"

"Not really," I admit. "It's just become a habit I enjoy. Is that weird?"

"No," she allows. "But you'll eventually need to learn to cope without so many."

I hesitate on whether I want to share why I really didn't scale down this week. Why I felt like I needed the extra support. Not because I felt like drinking, just in general.

That is, until I remember my promise to myself to stop feeling powerless and accept help.

"I saw Annika last weekend."

Dr. Marks' eyebrows fly up because she knows it's been something I've been avoiding. "And how did that go?"

"She's doing great. She's got a job at a lawyer's office, of all places," I tell her with a chuckle. "We talked about our dad."

She nods, leaning forward, clearly eager to hear more. "And?"

I uncross and recross my legs nervously. Talking about my feelings never gets easier, no matter how necessary it is. But Sherry Marks has helped me more than anyone ever has. She's got that concerned grandma vibe that never makes me feel judged. Something about her makes me feel safe letting it all out.

"I told her I felt guilty for leaving her there with just Erik. Especially since I know now how little he did to protect her."

"And you felt like that was your job."

I nod, a lump catching in my throat. "Yes."

"Even though you were only a child yourself?" There's that head tilt again.

The lump thickens and my eyes burn. "Yes."

"What did she say?"

I blink hard, staring down at my finger, which is now tracing circles into my thigh. "She said there's nothing to forgive, that what he did to us wasn't my fault. And even if I was there it wouldn't have stopped anything. But that if I needed her forgiveness, I had it."

A tear slips out and I wipe it away self-consciously.

Dr. Marks leans over and puts her hand over mine. "Did her forgiveness help?"

I look up, a little surprised at the question, though

I don't know why. She has a way of asking things I don't expect. Things that cut right to the issue.

"No," I admit. "Not even a little. Though I am glad she seems okay now."

Dr. Marks inhales slowly. "Because you've come so far in understanding the role the abuse played in your addiction and your relationships, I'm going to tell you something I think you're finally ready to hear."

I look at her warily, but I don't stop her like she says I always can if I need to. So she continues.

"Maybe it's not her forgiveness you really need," she offers softly with a squeeze of my hand. Then she withdraws, allowing me to hear that. To process that.

I rub circles into my jeans as I do. As I really absorb what she's suggesting.

"How can I forgive myself? Even if it wouldn't have made a difference, if I'd stayed …" I look up at the ceiling, blinking hard against the tears, swallowing against the lump in my throat. "At least she wouldn't have been alone."

"Like you would have felt alone?"

I look at Dr. Marks abruptly then. Because I know exactly what she's suggesting, the word she's used for that kind of thought process in the past — *projecting*. I'm projecting my trauma, the way I'd feel, onto Annika.

"Yes, that's exactly right," I reply.

"Did Annika say she felt alone?" Dr. Marks asks.

I shake my head. "No, she didn't. She always had a million friends. Even if she didn't tell them. Or couldn't tell them. She always had a place to go, people who liked her for her. I was the one who didn't have many friends. I was the one who missed Erik when he stopped hanging around the house so much. I was the one who always felt alone."

"So when you, a mere child yourself, ran away from the mental, emotional, and sexual abuse your own father committed against you, you felt guilty for leaving her. Because if she'd left you, you would have felt abandoned and alone."

"Yes," I admit. This time I don't wipe the tears away. What's the point?

"You feel like you failed your family."

I nod. "So as punishment, I failed myself?" It's not really a question. Because as I utter the words, I know without a doubt they're true.

Dr. Marks simply folds her hands in her lap and looks at me with equal parts compassion and encouragement.

She doesn't have to confirm the truth. That that's exactly what I did. I punished myself by behaving so recklessly that I pushed away everyone close to me while the drugs took me away from the deep chasm of hurt I was trying to escape. That I sought validation from people who couldn't know me, and therefore couldn't hurt me: the fans. They became everything while I subconsciously sabotaged my life.

And in doing that I also hurt my friends, my band. Maybe even because I *wanted* to hurt them. Maybe I wanted them to abandon me because I thought I deserved it for abandoning Annika. And this is all probably why I lied to Max too. Maybe deep down I wanted her to have a new reason to hate me, so she didn't get too close. Because god knows shit got real the moment I realized I'd fallen for her.

I really don't want to be this fucked up anymore. I want to know what it's like to be happy. To not run from my demons all the time.

"How do I just … change?" I ask, my mind still reeling. "How do I stop ruining everything I touch as penance for all the things I've done?"

"You've done the hardest part in recognizing the root of the problem."

"And the other part?"

"It's as simple and as hard as forgiving yourself."

And we're back here again. To something I have no clue how to do.

"How?" I say, a pleading note in the word.

She contemplates that for a moment. "Imagine Ward had been in this situation as a teen instead of you. Imagine he'd been abused by his father, as had his sister. Imagine if he'd left, then flagellated himself for it for years to the point of imploding his life spectacularly, until as an older adult he was finally able to start dealing with what had happened to him. Would you tell him to forgive himself in this situation?"

Oh, now she's just *trying* to make me cry. I sniff hard. As mad as I was at Ward a couple of months ago, I still consider him a brother. More so than my actual brother.

"I'd tell him he'd suffered enough. That he is good. That he is loved. That if he needs someone's forgiveness, he can have mine." I swallow hard, hanging my head, suddenly acutely aware of both why Annika said what she said as well as the point Dr. Marks is trying to make.

"And I'd tell you to take that big heart of yours and turn it toward yourself. You are good, Kristoffer. You are loved. But just like in the example with Ward, the person whose forgiveness you need before you can believe or accept anyone else's is your own."

I stare down into my hands, the occasional tear wetting my palms.

"When you're able to do that," Dr. Marks continues after a few minutes of silence, "you'll know how to move forward. You'll know who and what is really important to you, and you'll do what you can to make amends."

I clench my hands into fists and use them to rub at my eyes. "And if they don't want to hear it?"

Dr. Marks breathes a sigh out of her nose. "All you can do is try. You cannot control another's reactions. And if you truly accept that, you'll have peace no matter the outcome."

I continue to look down, realizing my right index finger has started tracing circles again. It's almost automatic now when I'm thinking, having long ago stopped being about the need to drink. That small thought makes me realize how far I've come. And how far I have yet to go.

Dr. Marks' words follow me home and haunt me into the evening.

As I'm getting ready for bed, I look up into the mirror. I look tired, but healthier than I have in a long time. And I'm ready to do this.

"I forgive you," I say to my reflection. With those words that are as true as the heart I'm about to lay on the line, tears blur my eyes. "I forgive you."

Eye of the Tiger by Survivor

West

When James opens his door, I have to admit, I panic a little. What if he's angry? What if he only let me come over to tell me off? What if, what if, what if.

Dr. Marks warned me not to do this and to remind myself that all I can do is try.

So when, without a word, James steps over his threshold and wraps his arms around me, I gotta admit, I wasn't expecting it.

"Hey, man," I joke, hugging him back.

He steps back and holds me at arm's length. "Fuck, it's good to see you, dude."

"*Daddy*," a tiny, chastising voice gasps from inside. James' four-year-old daughter, Zoe, appears in a purple tutu dress, wagging a finger and clutching a naked doll that has only half its hair. "That's a bad word."

James chuckles and tips his head, inviting me in. He leads me into the kitchen where his wife, Jeudi, is stirring something that smells incredible with one hand while propping their son, Zed, on her hip with the other.

"West," she greets me with a smile. "I was so glad to hear you called a meeting with the band." She leans forward and kisses me on the cheek. "You look good."

"And you look like a domestic goddess," I reply. "What is that amazing smell?"

She grins. "It's nothing fancy. Just pasta sauce," she says dismissively.

James shakes his head. "She's too modest. It's braised beef ragù," he says. "It's pretty much why I married her." He gives her a wink … which I'm hoping means he's joking.

The doorbell rings, interrupting any possible explanation, and James points down the hall.

"I'll get that. You can go hang in the studio, you know where it is," he tells me.

Nerves twist in my stomach, but all I do is smile and nod, waving at Jeudi as I head to James' studio.

It's a decently sized room with an upright piano in one corner and a couple of keyboards lined against the opposite wall. A few folding chairs sit around the couch on the back wall, ready for our little meeting.

It doesn't take long for James to appear, Nik and Michael in tow. Nik gives me a wary "hi" and Michael gives me a look. That's it. I guess I shouldn't be surprised. We've always been little more than band-mates, and he's usually the first to challenge me when I say or do something he doesn't like. He'll definitely be the hardest sell. They both settle onto the couch.

James starts to say something but is interrupt by Ward entering the room. His eyes meet mine solemnly, and I can see the battle on his face. Hug me or hit me? It's weird, but it makes me even happier to see him for some reason.

"Hey, man," I greet him quietly.

"Hey, West."

We stare at each other for a moment and I realize so much hinges on how he takes this. He's really the unspoken leader here.

I watch him as he sits down on the closest folding chair, draping a hand over his crossed legs. "So what did you call us here for?"

I puff out a sigh and take a seat in the folding chair across from him. James takes a seat next to Nik on the couch.

I look around at the faces of my band. My friends.

This is it. The moment of truth.

"I called you guys here to apologize. For real this time. And to prove it, there are some things I have to tell you first. Things that aren't easy for me to share."

My eyes flick up to Ward, who is now leaning his chin on his knotted fingers, his elbows propped on his knees. He and James both know about my childhood, but only Ward knows any details. But I know even Ward considered it the past, not understanding how much it still affected me. Not that I did until recently either.

So I tell them everything, sparing them the most explicit parts of the abuse I endured, but still giving them enough to leave them horrified and hanging on every word. Even, or perhaps especially, Ward.

I explain that all of my behavior since the moment I left home has been a result of it all, but I didn't realize it until I hit true rock bottom just over two months ago. That part they pretty much knew, of course.

"So my therapist, along with my meetings, have helped me understand why I've been self-sabotaging. And how to stop."

"And you think you can?" Ward asks.

"Yes," I say plainly, leaning back in my chair.

"Man," Michael says, his voice laced with awe. "I had no idea, dude." He shakes his head.

And it's the first time I think he's ever expressed any sort of empathy toward me.

"Well, it's not exactly something I just throw out there at dinner parties," I joke, trying to ease the tension of what I just laid on them. I look around at each of them in turn. "I didn't tell you guys for pity, though. I wanted you to understand what I've come to. That I felt guilt for all of that, and that's why I've been such a self-destructive asshole. I think I felt like someone should feel guilty, and fuck knows my dad clearly doesn't. But I realized it's not my cross to bear. It wasn't my fault. And now I can stop punishing myself for it and, by extension, everyone around me."

"You're like, all emotionally connected and shit now," Nik murmurs, watching me through narrowed eyes. "It's freaking me out a little."

I laugh, loud and honest. "It freaks me out a little too. But I feel so much better it's not even funny." I sigh, not sure this conversation is headed where I'd hoped but still feeling good about being honest with them. "So now you know. And I hope you also know that when I say I'm sorry this time, I mean it in a way I never could've before. I'm so fucking sorry for screwing this up for you guys. I know that doesn't undo anything, but I hope someday you can forgive me."

Michael looks at me. Really looks at me, in a way he never has before. "I had no fucking clue about any of this. I just thought you were an entitled asshole," he admits, and Ward snorts, presumably agreeing with the me-being-an-entitled-asshole part. Because, fair. "I mean, I can't say I'm not pretty fucking disappointed … but for what it's worth, I forgive you."

Nik nods slowly. "Same," she says nonchalantly. Michael gives her a sharp look, and she rolls her eyes. "All right, all right. I forgive you."

I smirk, knowing she probably considers it very un-rock-and-roll to get so mushy. Fuck knows I used to. But I'll take it.

I look to James next, who has had his hand over his mouth ever since I dropped the sexual-abuse bomb. He drops his hand, shaking his head.

"I had a clue, but even I didn't know how bad it was," he admits. His brown eyes soften as he meets mine. "It took a lot of strength for you to come here today. To tell us all that. Thank you."

"Don't thank me yet," I caution. "I'm just getting started."

James chuckles. "Well, you're doing a pretty good job of it, from where I'm sitting."

Ward raises an eyebrow at him and James shrugs.

"You guys are all a bunch of softies," Ward grumbles at them. But I can already tell by his tone that he's right there with them. He sighs heavily and swings his head to look at me. "Fine. I forgive you. But don't think I'm not going to make you show me you mean it after what you've put us through."

I grin widely, not blaming him in the slightest. "I'm glad you said that. Because I meant it when I said I'm just getting started. I hoped you'd all be ready to give me another chance, even though I know I don't deserve it. Because I've been working on something that you might be interested in."

Ward looks unimpressed, and I can tell he's a long way from forgetting my behavior. "We're listening."

"A concert. One so epic that it might just get us back in with everyone we've — *I've* burned."

James frowns. "And how are we going to do that when the label still holds the rights to all of our material?"

"I may have written new material," I respond. "Like, a whole album's worth of it."

Nik snorts. "You can write songs?"

"He's actually extremely talented," Ward breaks in, looking at me curiously. "Whose vocals did you write them for?"

I suppress a smile, his question outing that I've got

him hooked. "Yours, of course," I assure him. "Except one song."

"You're going to sing?" Ward asks hopefully.

"I'm going to sing." And even with all the progress I've made, something about saying those words unravels the last bit of fear coiled in my chest.

"Well, color me shocked. This could work," Ward murmurs.

"Why the one song?" Michael asks curiously.

I take a deep breath. "Because the rest of the songs are to get the fans and, hopefully, the label back on board. But my song? That one's for a girl. *The* girl. The one who started all of this. And she needs to know I haven't stopped thinking about her this whole damn time."

"You're in love with the reporter," Nik accuses me with a gasp.

I huff a laugh and nod. "Sure am."

Nik grins in response. "That's so fucking cute. I'm in."

"You've had a busy couple of months, haven't you?" James asks contemplatively.

I chuckle. "That I have."

A slow smile spreads over his face. "All right, kid. Let's hear this album of yours."

We Will Rock You by Queen

West

"No, you're still going early," I tell James. I replay the bridge, pausing at his cue. "Then you come in here."

James nods, so I keep going as he picks up on the cue, finally. At least, I hope he does. Ward watches on while trying to look like he isn't. I flick him a look and he grins, holding up his hands.

"Just keeping an eye on things," he says defensively. "We hit the recording studio Monday, after all."

"This is nothing," I assure him. "We're ready."

And we are. Still, I heave a sigh and set Rosie

aside. It's been an exhilarating — but exhausting — few weeks.

James continues to practice as I pack up for the day, and Ward sidles up to me.

"So. Recording next week at the good graces of our friendly L.A. indie rock network. Concert the Thursday after that, venue by the good graces of the stunning Frankie Greco and her towering intimidator of a husband. And Nik's girlfriend is on promo, sticking flyers to anything in L.A. that's not moving. Everything's falling into place. How about you? Got all your ducks in a row, West?" he asks. Except that's not what he's really asking.

"Nothing fell anywhere, we've been busting our asses 24/7," I point out. "And no, to answer the question you're really asking, I haven't talked to Jason about the article yet, you passive-aggressive jackass." I say it with a laugh, because I'm mostly teasing him. "But I'm meeting him for a drink tomorrow night."

Ward tries to look cool, but I can tell he's relieved. He's so tightly wound sometimes, I wish he'd find a girl he cares about as much as I care about Maxi. Because there's nothing like a woman who makes you want to be a better version of yourself.

And that makes me remember … fuck, I miss Maxi. I've tried not to think too hard about it these past few months, but this is all because of her. Don't get me wrong, getting my shit together was for me. But this concert? This apology? It's for her. I mean, if it gets the fans and the label back, great. At this point, though, I honestly couldn't give a shit.

Because, shockingly enough, my self-worth no longer hinges on the whims of the masses. And thank fucking god for that.

But a life without Maxi Marshall? That's like Simon without Garfunkel. Hall without Oates. Jimmy Page without Robert Plant. In other words, unthinkable.

Still, I put off the meeting with Jason because this is the part I'm most nervous about. What if he won't go along with what I have in mind? What if he tells her?

I shake my head as I zip Rosie back into her case. Dr. Marks is right. If I'm not careful, I'm going to what-if myself into an early grave.

With a chuckle, I head home with the hope that I'll find something to distract me until tomorrow evening.

♪

DISTRACTIONS OR NO, TIME MARCHES ON, AND Saturday evening finds me entering a café near *Rock Scene*'s office, looking for Jason.

I spot him at a table near the back, and I glance

around nervously at the packed room. I should've thought this through a little better. The whole point was to keep this on the down-low. Not just from Maxi, either.

I slide into the seat across from Jason, his eyes landing on me in surprise.

"You showed," he remarks.

I smirk. "Yep. I did."

He nods. "All right then. I'm going to guess this little meeting has something to do with the buzz that Violent Mood Swings is putting on a concert in a couple weeks?"

I'm secretly pleased that he knows. That means our grassroots marketing plan is working.

"Sort of," I admit. "But it's also sort of about the fact that I created a shitstorm for you guys a couple months back. And I'd like to make amends for that."

Jason arches an eyebrow, disbelief written all over his face.

"Is this another 'apology'?" he asks, with air quotes and all.

I laugh, despite myself. "Cute. I'm pretty sure saying 'I'm sorry' would go over like a lead balloon at this point," I reply. "So I'm here to offer you an exclusive."

Jason snorts. "Well, I have to admit everyone's

curious how and why you guys might be getting back together. What exactly will you give us?"

I smile, spreading my hands out. "Everything, Jason. The whole story, from cradle to grave to rising again."

"Still think you're God, do you?" There's no humor in his voice.

I realize it did come out sounding like that, especially since the version of me he knows is pre-rock-bottom.

"I like to think of it more like a phoenix rising from the ashes," I offer. "Don't you want to be the magazine that reveals why I burned it all to the ground?"

Despite himself, I can tell he's intrigued. And I know he can't afford to pass up this opportunity.

"When do you want it to run?"

"As soon as possible."

He considers. "I can get it online within a few days of you sitting down with Max. But print doesn't go out until the day before the concert."

"I'm not looking for publicity," I tell him. "And I don't want Maxi on this particular article. Hell, I'm pretty sure she'd tell you exactly where you could stick this interview if you even asked her."

Jason snorts a laugh. "Yep, that sounds about

right," he agrees. "Though I don't blame her for being pissed at you."

"You don't know the half of it," I reply. "Which is where my only condition comes in."

He folds his arms over his chest with a dubious expression, one that says he was waiting for the catch.

"I want to do the article for two reasons: First, to give you guys the edge back and hopefully put to rest any doubts about your involvement with the lies I told. Second, to show a certain feisty-as-hell reporter that I'm not fucking around this time," I explain. "That's why someone else needs to do the article. So it gets printed. So she sees me laying it all out there."

"And the condition?"

"I want her to cover the concert."

Jason narrows his eyes. "Why?"

I frown. "Does it matter?"

"She's like a little sister to me so, yes, it matters. I'm not sending her there so you can publicly humiliate her."

"You've got the wrong end of this, man," I respond with a grin. "Because it's all about publicly humiliating myself. And then making sure she damn well knows how I feel about her."

Jason leans forward on the table, looking at me intently. And he does have that big brother "I'm going to beat your ass if you fuck with her" vibe going.

"And how do you feel about her?"

I rub my lips together. If she hasn't told him anything, I'm not sure whether it's a betrayal of her trust to. But then, as far as I know, she doesn't reciprocate my feelings anyway. And I've probably got a snowball's chance in hell with this woman. But for Maxi, I'll take those odds.

"I'm in love with her," I admit quietly. "Even if she doesn't love me back. I need her to know. I need to show her how fucking sorry I am."

"You sure about this? Because from where I'm standing, I'm pretty sure she's hated your guts for years."

I smile sadly, still hoping that's not true. Still willing to take the chance.

"What do I have to lose that I haven't already lost?"

25

Missing You by John Waite

Max

"Max?" Alexsis's voice draws my gaze to the door. "Do you have a minute to look over an article for the website before it goes to Jason?"

I pull a face. "That'll take more than a minute." I throw my pen down with a sigh and gesture for her to hand it to me. "But for you, of course."

She hands me the small sheaf of papers nervously, settling down in the extra chair in my cubicle.

"You're going to watch me read it?" I ask dryly.

She shrugs. "I just … thought you might want to discuss it with me while you go."

I furrow my brow. "You know if I have to ask you questions, it's not ready for Jason, right?"

"I know." Alexsis bobs her head, and her nervous energy is weirding me out.

I fight the urge to pull a face, unsure what's up with her today but assuming she just needs reassurance. "Well, you're a talented writer, I'm sure it's fine," I mumble as my eyes start to scan the page.

But I only take in the headline before my eyes snap back up to hers, suddenly understanding her nerves.

"What the fuck is this?" I ask plainly, dropping the pages on my desk like they're on fire.

"Just read it. Please?"

"This is an interview with Kristoffer fucking Westberg, Alexsis. When did you do this?" I demand. "*Why* did you do this?" Even I can hear the hurt in my voice. She knows this subject is off-limits.

"You'll understand when you read it. And you need to read it," she urges. "Trust me."

I snort. "Trust you. Like I trusted West?"

"It's okay to be mad at him. But this is going live, and it's going to be a big deal. I figured it was better if you read it before everyone else. So you weren't unprepared."

I furrow my brow and frown. I hate to admit it, but

she has a point. The last thing I need is to be blind-sided by West again.

"Fine," I snap, snatching the pages back. "But I don't have to like it."

Alexsis presses her lips together and her nostrils flare. She's clearly trying not to laugh at my petulant attitude. Because I know I'm being a little over the top, it almost snaps me out of my funk. Almost.

But as soon as I start reading, the funk is back in full force.

Until it's replaced by my stomach dropping into my shoes. And maybe a tear or two. And a hand over my mouth.

When I finish, I gently place the pages down and lean back in my chair.

"He really told you all of that?" I ask in a whisper. But I already know the answer. Of course he did. How else would she know?

She nods. "Yep. I think it was harder on me, actually. He seemed surprisingly okay talking about the whole thing."

I shake my head. "It seems like an odd publicity stunt and totally not like West to share all that. But then, I guess they need all the help they can get ahead of whatever farce of a concert they intend to put on next week."

"So you know it's all the truth?"

My eyes meet hers. "Why? Do you not believe him?" I ask curiously.

"That's not what I meant, but yes, I believe him. He's ... different."

I snort. "If I didn't know this" — I pick up the article — "was all true, that statement alone would make me think this whole thing is an act. Then again, the publicity stunt angle still fits, even if it is true. Why else would he do this?" I drop the article back on the desk, disgusted.

"Oh, Max. Isn't it obvious?"

I level a don't-go-there look at her. "No. It's not. Not to me at least. But I also don't give a shit."

Alexsis gives me a look filled with pity. She hesitates. "It's okay to miss him, Max. Even though he hurt you."

Indignation tingles over every inch of my skin. "I do *not* miss him," I scoff.

Alexsis's expression turns to exasperation. "Oh really? Then why have you been sulking around for the last three months doing google searches and scanning social media for news about him when you think nobody's looking?"

My eyes go wide at being called out and my face flushes. "I'm not sulking! And that was just ... morbid curiosity," I stammer defensively.

God, I'm so lame.

I've totally been sulking.

I totally miss him.

I'm a stupid, stupid woman who is obviously a glutton for punishment. What he did … it went beyond potentially trashing my career, which thankfully has mostly recovered. He trashed my trust. Again.

And I shouldn't worry about him. I shouldn't look for him in every headline. I shouldn't want to know what the band's doing back together and what's going on with this concert. I shouldn't love him.

Because that leads to only one place: more heartbreak.

But … what if everything he was quoted as saying in the article is true? I rifle through to the last page, trying to remember exactly how he worded his response to Alexsis asking why he was sharing all of this. When I find it, I realize I'd merely skimmed it the first time.

"Because this time, it's real. And to prove that, I need to set right what I did wrong. At least, as much as people will let me. But I also get I may not deserve that in some people's eyes. And that's okay too."

On a second, closer read, I wonder … he couldn't have been talking about me … could he? Tears prickle at the backs of my eyes, and I blink rapidly to contain them. On some level I want to believe it's the truth.

But even if it's his truth, does it change anything? Trust isn't so easily rebuilt. Even he gets that.

I look up to find Alexsis watching me. "I'm not supposed to tell you this, but Jason's going to ask you to cover the concert. You don't have to interview the band or anything, just go. I thought you might like a chance to think about that *not* in front of your boss."

She rises, making to leave.

"Alexsis, wait," I call after her.

She turns back to me and I offer her the printed article. "Here."

"I meant for you to keep that one," she says softly.

I sigh heavily. "Thank you," I murmur.

And she knows I don't mean for the printout, because she gives me a sad smile, then leaves.

After she's gone, I contemplate reading the article again, now that I've calmed down a little. And maybe I should. Maybe I should take off the bitter filter I've been viewing the world through lately.

But then again, maybe I need to look at it that way because the truth is so much scarier. Risks always are. And West is a risk I can't imagine myself taking ever again.

26

———

I Won't Back Down by Tom Petty & The Heartbreakers

West

Preshow jitters rarely used to be an issue for me. Maybe it was the drugs and alcohol. Or maybe I was high on the energy of the crowd, the adoration of the fans.

Or maybe no show has ever mattered quite like this one.

Six days ago, I exposed myself to the world. Digitally, as it were, not in the perverted way. Though I have been known to do that in the past.

But no, this time it wasn't physically. This time everyone knows my story. Facts and happenings I tried hard to ignore for most of my adult life. It's all out there now, and the show sold out not long after. So clearly people are curious. Hopefully some even show up for the actual music.

Either way, today I expose the only part of me I didn't in that article: my heart. Today is my grand gesture. My *Say Anything* moment. Except instead of a boombox, I've got Rosie, a kickass sound system courtesy of Baltia, and an epic ballad written expressly for one Maxi Marshall to end what I hope will be an equally epic evening.

But first, I've gotta get there. And fuck if today didn't make me miss having our own crew. Fortunately, the backbreaking work of lugging all our gear into the club, setting up, and doing soundchecks kept me from thinking too hard most of the day. But we're minutes to doors open now, and there's nothing to distract me from the swirling pit of nerves in my stomach. I should've gone with the rest of the band to get something to eat ahead of the show, but I have zero appetite. And I don't want to have something in my stomach to throw up if the nerves win. God, the nerves.

They've been made worse by not knowing how Maxi took the article, or if she even read it at all. And while Jason said he'd "do his best" to get her here …

well, not knowing if she'll show is another level of torture I was unprepared for.

I feel the equipment crate I'm sitting on shift and a voice to my right says, "So I hear tell from Ward this show isn't just about getting your career back."

I huff a breath out of my nose and turn. "It's still a trip seeing you without crazy-colored hair," I say.

Frankie grins over at me, tugging at her now-dark-brown locks, though at least she's still wearing the bright red lipstick she's famous for. A few years ago I was a falling rock star when she was a new, unknown face on the rock scene. She'd just bought Baltia, but now she's a legend in her own right for what she's done with it and several other clubs since.

"It's a trip seeing you sober," she shoots back with a teasing note to her voice. "So is it true? Is this really about a girl?"

"Yep," I admit, not knowing what to add that won't make me even more nervous than I already am.

"And you love her?" she pushes.

"Yep." I inhale deeply to calm myself. I'm not sure I've admitted that out loud to anyone but Maxi before, but Frankie has a way of eliciting honesty. Doesn't hurt that she's intimidating as hell.

Frankie is silent for a beat, assessing me.

"Is she why you cleaned up your act?"

I smile. "In a way," I respond truthfully. "She was

the kick in the ass. Getting sober? Owning my shit? That was for me."

Another beat of silence passes. "Damn, West, that's some deep shit right there. Never thought I'd see the day. But I'm happy for you."

"Thanks. How's it looking out there?"

"Line's not just around the damn block — I'm pretty sure it stretches all the way to Hollywood and Highland," she replies with a grin. "One way or another, you're making rock history tonight."

I laugh. "No pressure, though, right?"

"Fuck yes, there's pressure," she responds matter-of-factly, rising. "But you're wicked talented." She looks down at me. "And you've got a true heart. You have no idea how rare that is. Trust me." She claps me on the shoulder. "You'll be fine. Now put on your big girl panties and let's do this fucking thing."

I shake my head and laugh. Trust Frankie to light a fire under my ass. I rise, retrieving Rosie from her stand backstage. I never leave her onstage because I always need to kiss her for luck before a show, which I do. Been a long time. And even though it's not the tour I thought I'd get, I'm happy to play music for a crowd again. I test a few chords, and her gentle hum soothes the raging inferno in my gut. Let's do this fucking thing, indeed.

Distantly, I hear the doors open and the crowd

pour in. Drink orders start to be called so loudly I can hear them from backstage. Chairs scrape. Feet thunder down the stairs to the stage pit. This is fucking happening.

A few minutes before showtime, the band regroups backstage, and at Ward's direction we huddle, arms slung over each other's shoulders in a circle. There's no opening act, so we're going to be up very soon. As we silently embrace, we listen to the volume in the club ramp up as people cram in.

With a squeeze of Ward's hand on my shoulder, he breaks the huddle. "All right, fuckers. What are we gonna do tonight?" he asks, first pointing at James.

"Play like no one is watching," James replies with a grin. Ward rolls his eyes and points to Nik, next in the circle.

"Go balls to the wall," Nik says.

Now Michael rolls his eyes. "Girls don't even have balls," he groans.

Nik points at her tits. "I believe it was Joan Jett who said it best — 'Girls have got balls. They're just a little higher up, that's all.'"

I chuckle as Ward shakes his head and points to Michael.

"Make mama proud," he says.

He's such a mama's boy, so I'm thoroughly unsurprised. Ward smirks at Michael but doesn't say anything, he just moves his hand to point at me.

"I gotta see about a girl," I say.

Ward stares at me and slaps a hand on my shoulder. "You are one sappy motherfucker, West."

Nik looks confused. James laughs at the expression on her face.

"Give her a break," I tell him. "I'm pretty sure she was like two when that movie came out."

"What movie?" Nik asks blankly. James, Ward, and I all crack up.

But before we can fill her in, out on the stage, Frankie takes the mic and starts hyping up the crowd. A hush falls over the band, and not just to hear her talk. That Frankie herself is introducing us … well, it drives it home how epic this is.

When she cues us to take the stage, my adrenaline starts pumping. We enter side stage and the crowd goes fucking apeshit. Cheers, calls, hands reaching, bodies pressing toward the stage, the whole nine yards. From what I can see under the bright lights, the place is crammed wall to wall.

I grin over at Ward as I plug Rosie into her amp and he takes the mic. And without preamble, Michael cues us in and the music explodes through the club.

We picked a fast, hard song to start, and it was hands down the right choice. The energy level in the place is palpable, and I give everything up to the music. I'm home. All of my worries, gone, surrendered to the melody.

We finish the first song and go straight into our second, taking the tempo back a bit. The crowd is loving it, and I gotta admit, I'm relieved. While my songs aren't *totally* different, it's definitely not our usual sound either. I don't know how Ward constantly puts himself out there writing songs that people may very well shit all over. I'm just glad that doesn't seem to be happening tonight.

As we start a third song, though, the tenor of the crowd changes in a way I didn't expect as a surge of bodies presses people closer to the stage. I look over at Ward, who looks back at me with a shake of the head. Neither of us may know why, but something just shifted.

We keep going, but the masses are now making some very different noises. A movement side stage catches my eye. Nils has come onto the fucking stage and is yelling in Ward's ear.

My stomach drops and Ward motions for us to stop, which we do immediately, plunging the club into rumbles of confusion. Bodies press more frantically at the base of the stage. With the light up I can see people crammed into every nook and cranny, and things are starting to get … shovey. I look back nervously at Nils, and it's then that I notice a cop and a fireman behind him as he takes the mic.

"Everyone please, stay calm," Nils urges. I pale as the crowd starts booing. He waves his hands, but they don't quiet down. "Unfortunately, the police and fire marshal are shutting the concert down." At that, the crowd goes insane, and not in the good way. There's jeering and loud booing and a few people throwing things as the shoving starts to get more violent.

For a split second I wonder if I should be afraid. But then Frankie strides quickly up to the mic, her husband not far behind. She's got presence, but this guy … he's a wall of dark, muscled terror if I've ever seen one. And the sight of the two of them looking like hell's fury is enough to quiet the place.

"Look, we're sorry, but you can thank the horde of gatecrashers who thought it would be cute to rush security, who then had to call the cops to contain it. Please, for the love of fucking Christ, cooperate and you'll receive a flyer at the door that'll tell you how to get your money back."

Frankie steps back, but her husband stays in place, glaring at the crowd. There's plenty of grumbling as everyone turns back toward the stairs, pushing toward the exit, but no challenges to the enforcer watching them go. They're distinctly more orderly. And if I weren't so freaked out right now, it might almost be funny.

"What the fuck just happened?" I ask, joining Ward, Frankie, and Nils at center stage, Nik and Michael following close behind.

Nils frowns. "We were already oversold when a group of assholes without tickets decided to just push their way in. It was only about a dozen people, but then *everyone* in line behind them decided to jump in on the action," he replies, disgust lacing his tone. "We had extra security, but there was no way we could've stopped them. I'm pretty sure half the fucking city was still waiting outside hoping to see the show. So even after the police got here, it took a few minutes for them to even be able to get in. I had to bring them in the goddamn side door. Then the fire marshal showed up and didn't even give us the option to thin the crowd. He just declared it over."

Frankie throws us all an apologetic look. "Sorry, guys. If I'd have known the line was that bad, I would've dealt with it before we got started."

I shake my head. "It's not your fault a bunch of assholes ruined it, but thanks anyway." As the implications of the show being shut down sink in, I remember the only part of this that mattered in the first place. "Oh fuck." I look up at Ward. "Maxi."

Ward purses his lips. "We don't even know if she was here, dude."

"Maxi … you mean Max Marshall?" Nils asks.

"Yeah, you know her?"

"Of course. You introduced us, remember? At the private fan concert?"

I want to smack myself in the forehead. Duh. "Did you see her tonight?"

"Sure did."

A warm feeling spreads through my chest. She came. That's something. A new plan starts forming in my head. But then I look at my bandmates.

Ward snorts. "Don't worry about us. This shit happens. Bright side? This is going to be big news. And with the crowd that was here tonight? We're going to have zero problems rescheduling. At a bigger venue though, maybe." He shrugs apologetically Frankie's way. She waves a hand dismissively back.

"Are you sure? Because you guys are important to me too, and I don't want you to think —"

"Fuck, would you just go get the girl already?" Michael cuts in, exasperated.

A wide grin breaks over my face. "Thanks, guys." And then my face falls. "Shit, my driver is busy until later because I thought I'd be here."

"Where do you need to go?" The deep voice rumbles out of Frankie's husband, and the hairs on my arms stand up. I give Frankie a look and she smiles slyly.

"Culver City," I respond.

"You bringing that?" he asks in return, pointing at Rosie.

"Shit, no." I slide the strap over my head and hand her to Ward.

"You're leaving your guitar behind?" he asks, his eyebrows shooting up.

"I don't have time to argue, just take her," I insist.

"How are you going to play her song without your guitar?" James asks.

"I don't need the guitar," I assure them.

Ward takes Rosie, holding her delicately. So delicately I almost laugh. But I don't have time for that shit.

"Can you drive fast?" I ask Frankie's husband.

He raises one, thick eyebrow, but it's Frankie who answers. "Don't worry, West. Julian's got you covered."

27

In Your Eyes by Peter Gabriel

Max

"Well, that was insane," Alexsis says as we take a seat in a pie shop just down the block from Baltia.

"I assume you're referring to the concert and not your choice of cereal on pie," I reply, gesturing at the Froot Loops-laden concoction sitting in front of her.

She grins. "You clearly haven't tried it," she replies, then points at my chocolate brownie pie slice. "Chocolate is boring and predictable. This is surprising and exciting."

I grimace. "I'll stick with my chocolatey silky deliciousness, thanks."

She shrugs. "Suit yourself." She takes a bite of pie, looking so sublimely happy I have to chuckle. "So, of the little we saw, what did you think?"

I shrug back. "It was all right." Such a lie. It was many things, but just "all right" wasn't one of them. "Thanks for coming with me. Even if I didn't end up having to talk to him, I'm glad you were there."

"Of course. I'm glad I went. I love their new sound. Shame it was such a freaking circus it got shut down early."

"Yes, well, clearly they underestimated what a circus it would be. And they do seem to have gone a new direction," I reply.

Alexsis rolls her eyes. "All right, Max. Can we drop the polite chatter? I can tell you're totally shook right now."

I raise an eyebrow and shoot her a smirk that could rival West's. Because even though she's considerably younger than me at twenty-two, I'm pretty sure "shook" isn't a thing anymore. She sticks her tongue out at me in response and I laugh.

"Fine, yes, I'm 'shook.' Are you happy?" I reply.

"Are you?" she returns. "Happy, I mean?"

"Not really."

"Then me neither."

I snort. "While I appreciate the solidarity, I really

don't want to talk about it." I take a large bite of pie so I can avoid doing exactly that.

"If you say so. But I think you'd feel better if you got it off your chest." She takes a bite of her own pie, clearly thinking while she chews. "You can't tell me seeing him up there wasn't …" She shudders theatrically for effect.

I suck in a sharp breath and close my eyes against the memory. The image of him up there on stage.

"Yes, fine, it was fucking hot," I allow. I'm not sure how I could forget what it feels like to watch him up there. It's a mix of awe and lust that's hard to ignore.

"And you're sure you can never forgive him?"

"I don't remember him asking since he's decided he's all fixed up this time around."

"I don't remember you giving him a chance to."

I tap my fork on the plate. "Fine, all right? Seeing him made me realize that if he asked I probably would. Because it was one thing to be mad at him when I didn't have to see him. But I'm not totally oblivious to the fact that Kristoffer Westberg is one-hundred-percent my kryptonite. As soon as I saw him tonight, I remembered that. So I'm just thanking god that shit all got shut down before he had a chance to invite me backstage or something."

"You say that like it's a bad thing," she points out.

"He's a ticking time bomb of emotional wreck-age," I snap back.

"I dunno. Seems like he might really have his shit together this time."

"No, that's just the West effect working on you too. One interview and bam," I slam my hand down on the table between us. "Off melt the panties. Then you're groupie putty in his capable smoking-hot-guitarist hands."

"Well, you'd know firsthand how capable they are," she points out with a grin.

I scrunch my face up. "That part I do miss," I admit. "The crazy West-coaster? Not so much."

"Even if he has —"

"Changed? Come on, Alexsis. You're not *that* young. You don't get with a guy expecting him to change. Besides, even if he has, he's still a rock star."

She finishes eating her last bite of pie in silence, then carefully sets down her fork.

"Even if he is, it's all in how you choose to see it. And what I see is a guy trying to make things right with his band and the woman he —"

"So help me god, do not say 'loves.'"

"I don't have to — he already did, remember?"

"Oh I remember," I reply with a hard edge to my voice. "That's the problem. Letting him love me would be —"

"Dangerous? Crazy? Just what you need?" Alexsis interrupts.

I frown. "I wasn't going to say any of those things," I respond defensively. Except I *was* going to say something pretty similar to the first two.

"Yeah, it's annoying when people interrupt you, isn't it?" she points out blithely, taking a sip of water. "And do you know why you keep interrupting me?"

I roll my eyes. "Why?" I ask dryly.

"Because you're *afraid*." She shakes her head slowly. "To think, the woman who I look up to. My role model. Afraid of taking a chance on love."

"I've already taken too many chances on West," I point out.

She tilts her head to the side and scrutinizes me. "But isn't that what loving someone is? Taking a chance every single day that they'll stick around? That the rug won't get pulled out from under you? Because I'm just not buying the 'he's a rock star' angle. You're a goddamn rock journalist for Christ's sake. Lame excuse, if you ask me."

And my eyebrows are so high I'm pretty sure they're about to pop off my forehead. "Well, tell me what you really think, why don't you?" She grins at me. And then I add softly, "I'm your role model?"

Her smile relaxes into something sweeter. "Yes. Even though you're kind of being a hypocrite right now. What, you want to get close to the rock life but never be affected by it? Not gonna happen, sister. Give in. You want him. He wants you. Everything else is just … stuff. You'll figure it out. I know you can. Because you're a badass, and you're not my role model for nothing."

My heart aches at her words. She's actually completely right. And hearing it that way makes me realize, I'm not just afraid of West because I love him.

"But what if you're wrong?" I ask, swallowing hard against the lump in my throat. Preparing to voice a fear I didn't even realize I had until now. Until she pushed me to look closer. "What if now that he's got his life back he realizes his feelings for me weren't real? That they were just a part of all the fucked up emotions he was working through?"

"Why would you think that?" she asks, her voice filled with exasperation.

That ache in my heart swells. "He hasn't talked to me in more than three months. He asked *you* to write the article. And he didn't even invite me to the concert, Jason had to tell me to go. If he wanted to see me, if he wanted *me* … well, this is West we're talking about. The man's not exactly shy about going after what he wants."

I look down, blushing hard. God, I had no clue

what really lay under all my anger and fear was plain old insecurity.

"So you're saying you would take him back, you just don't think he wants you?" Alexsis asks.

I look up, tears now swimming in my eyes. "Yeah, I guess that's what I'm saying. Is that messed up? To want someone you thought you were pissed off at — and for good reason — but turns out you were just afraid they didn't really want you back?"

"Yeah, actually, that's pretty messed up," she admits.

I laugh, and a tear slips out.

"Well, if he doesn't realize how fucking awesome you are, then it's his loss," she says, lifting her chin.

"Exactly," I agree. "I say good riddance West, and bring on more pie."

"If you can actually eat another piece of pie after that, you really are my role model," Alexsis jokes.

I look down at the crumbs left on my plate and glance at my watch. I'm pretty sure they're closing soon, not that I think I could actually eat another piece right this second anyway.

"Eh. Maybe a piece to go," I agree.

Alexsis laughs. "Sounds good to me."

We rise, heading for the counter, but I stop her with a hand on her arm.

"Thanks, Alexsis."

She smiles back at me and puts her hand on mine to give it a squeeze. "Anytime."

"And you know I've got your back the next time you need to moan over some idiot who doesn't know what he's got," I assure her as we wait for the counter girl.

"Well, here's hoping I find that idiot soon. Pie can only keep a girl happy for so long," she teases airily.

As my ride drops me off at my apartment building way earlier and way more sober than I'd planned on being, I'm somehow thankful for my life right now. As crappy as the last few months have felt, I truly have a lot of good things going. My career. My family. My friendships. Love lost isn't the end; it can always be found again if you're open to it.

It's a thought that brings a sad smile to my face as I walk through the open wrought iron gate into the courtyard, the August night air warm and dry. And even though I know I shouldn't wonder, I do. What's West doing right now? Is he upset about the concert being shut down? Is he burying his disappointment in some groupie?

Ugh. That last thought makes me shudder in

disgust. I look up as I approach the arched entry door to the building itself.

And the answer to my question sits on the top step. My breath catches in my throat as West rises, slowly descending the steps to stand in front of me. He looks exactly as he did onstage in his uniform tight back tee and dark wash jeans. Except his dark eyes looked tired and a five o'clock shadow is starting to bud on his strong jaw. Everything about him, perfect and imperfect, makes my heart pound in my chest.

"Hey, Maxi."

I want to close my eyes against the swell of emotion his voice brings in me. I can feel the tears in my eyes. And everything I knew I'd feel around him floods me at once. Loss so deep it tears me open. Love so strong it heals. Hope that grates too sharply on the jagged edges of my heart.

"What are you doing here, West?"

His eyes search mine, dark and intense. He smells like sweat and guitar strings, heaven and hell, salvation and damnation.

"You went to the concert," he says.

My brows pull together at his non-answer. "Yes …?"

"I didn't know if you would. But I figured it was more likely if it wasn't me who asked."

My mouth pops open. "Jason … but … that was

really you?" As soon as the stuttered accusation is out of my mouth I realize it may not make much sense.

But he nods anyway. "I didn't think you wanted to talk to me. So I had this whole plan."

"To get me to cover your comeback concert?" I ask.

"Yes," he admits, shoving his hands in his pockets. "But mostly to play the song I wrote for you."

My eyebrows jump. "You wrote me a song?"

"Yep. And I came here to sing it to you. But now that I'm here, that feels all wrong."

My heart lurches at the thought that I may not get to hear this song, one I didn't even know about until a minute ago.

"You wrote me a song," I say again, softer, breathier.

One of his hands pops out of his pockets, starting to reach … until he stops it, clenching it into a fist and letting it drop to his side.

"I did. Actually, I wrote a whole album because of you. Went to therapy for the first time since rehab because of you. I'm standing here, the closest to whole I've ever been … because of you, Maxi. And I could sing you a song. But I think just telling you is better. No flash. No theatrics. Just the truth."

My breathing stutters. "And what's that?" I whisper.

"That I'm not going to be completely whole without you." He loses the battle with his hand, and he reaches up to cup my face. His fingers send warmth skating over my skin and running down my spine. "You speak truth. You don't back down from a challenge. You don't hide behind lies under the guise of doing what you think you have to. You're beautiful, and strong, and you don't take shit from anyone, especially not me. And I think I've loved you from the moment you told me there were more important people than you who needed my apology. It's just took me a while to realize that wasn't true. There's nobody more important than you. Not to me."

"You can't possibly mean that." My voice wavers as I fight a losing battle against the tears in my eyes.

He smiles softly, stroking his thumb over my cheek.

"But I do. You showed me what I'd let myself become. And that I couldn't stop hiding from it anymore. You were the only one who knew every awful thing about me. And you still chose me. I thought I'd never forgive myself for lying to you, for ruining what we might have had."

I tilt my head into his palm, and he runs his fingers down my jaw.

"But you did?" I prompt.

"I did," he confirms. "Turns out I needed to learn

to forgive myself to give myself permission to be loved. And, you know, to not be a complete asshole."

A laugh escapes me. "You're not a complete asshole."

He scrunches his nose and tips his head back and forth. "I really was, though."

We both laugh, and the tears finally find their way out. I brush them away self-consciously.

"And the other part?" I ask, not wanting to use the word "love." It all feels like too much right now.

"It's why I'm here," he says plainly.

I press my lips together and look up into his eyes, fighting against thinking too hard about all of the broken pieces inside of me.

"Why don't you come up and we'll talk," I offer, taking a step back.

His hand falls and he shoves it back in his pocket, nodding slowly. "Cool."

He follows me inside and up the stairs.

The minute it takes me to fumble for my keys and get the door open make me feel like a teenager sneaking her boyfriend into her room. Except I'm far from the teenager who mooned over him. Now I'm the woman whose heart and mind are still more at odds than I'd like them to be.

Once we're inside, I gesture to the beat-up tan leather couch dominating the small living room.

"Want a drink?" I offer as I kick off my shoes.

But West is having none of it. He slides his hand over mine, tugging me toward him. I allow him to draw me in front of him but not too close. I stare up at him warily.

"Am I too late? Are you seeing someone else?" he murmurs.

"No," I say, my mouth going dry. "And no."

The left side of his lips tip up. "You know, the last time I said this, it didn't go over well."

Nerves tumble in my tummy. "Lies and love don't tend work together in the same conversation," I reply delicately.

His brows pinch together. "I'm sorry for lying to you. For disappointing you, again. I promise you, I am doing everything in my power to be the man you deserve."

The war between me and my brokenness ceases. Because the truth in his words is undeniable. But more so is how I feel about him. The chance I can't not take. And maybe he's exactly what I need to heal my heart.

"I believe you. That article, West ... that was unbelievable."

His gaze softens. "I'm glad you read it. After everything I did, it was the only thing I could think of to even begin to explain — much less expect — forgiveness."

"But that's why you did it, isn't it?"

He shakes his head adamantly. "I don't need the forgiveness of strangers. I need the forgiveness of the people I love." He pauses, his eyes tightening with worry. "Will you forgive me?"

"I forgive you," I reply, almost automatically. Because I realize I already had. I've always known who he is deep down. And this time it really does feel like he's on the right path, finally. "But you're going to have to keep showing me."

He smirks. "I have a few ways in mind," he replies huskily.

My breath hitches at the glint in his eye. "Oh yeah?" I ask, barely above a whisper. "Like what?"

He draws me into his arms, dipping his forehead to meet mine. "Like telling you the truth. Always," he promises. He pulls back and stares deeply into my eyes. "I love you, Max Marshall."

A slow smile spreads over my face. He called me *Max*. I don't point it out, but the gravity of it underscores his declaration like his subconscious is making promises to take this seriously too. If I'd had any doubts left whether he was worth the risk, they'd be gone. But I don't.

"And then what?" I ask teasingly, running my hands down his chest.

He cocks an eyebrow. "Well, I was going to save fucking you for later, but if you insist." And without hesitation, he leans forward and flips me over his shoulder, carrying me toward the bedroom.

I squeal with surprised laughter. "Holy shit, West!"

He walks into the bedroom and drops me on the bed, climbing over me. Before I can even catch my breath, his mouth lands on mine, his lips pushing my mouth open, his tongue invading my senses. Heat and desire pool between my thighs and I moan into his mouth.

He makes to pull away, but I put my hands on his face.

"I love you too, Kristoffer Westberg," I breathe.

His face draws together in an expression somewhere between relief and delight before his mouth is on mine again, his hands pulling at my clothing. And I'm right there with him, until we're both naked, until he's worshipping every inch of my body.

His mouth trails down my chest, leaving a blazing trail of kisses that spread heat across my skin. His thumbs circle my nipples as his mouth goes lower, his teeth against the sensitive plane of my lower stomach creating a sharp contrast to his hot, silky tongue that sends jolts of pleasure shooting through my core.

And when his lips land on my inner thighs, I whimper with anticipation. His hands leave my breasts to join his mouth and as his tongue works my clit while he slides two fingers deep inside me, I arch off the bed.

"Oh my god," I groan. "Yes."

He pumps with his fingers. "I love hearing you, Maxi."

He speeds up and I lose my words. With a grin I can feel rather than see, his tongue returns to the mix, lapping in circles and sending me into a frenzy. I come hard and fast, pushing into his mouth as I grip the bedspread under me.

When the white hot fire of my orgasm starts to recede from my limbs, I push up. First to my elbows, watching him rise between my legs. And when his hard, ready cock comes into view, I push up to fully sitting, taking him in my mouth with the fervor that only post-orgasmic bliss can induce.

I spare him nothing, shoving his silky length deep into my throat as I suck hard, using one hand to follow my mouth up and down as the other massages him lower. His hands fist into my hair as he groans and pushes through my lips to the rhythm I've set. I relax, silently begging him to fuck my mouth. And he does.

God, the noises he makes. Deep groans that reverberate through him. I'm so wet and worked up I can barely stand it. I feel him tighten in my palm an instant before he pulls out of my mouth.

I look up at him, licking my lips as he sucks in a breath through his teeth.

"You are so fucking sexy," he tells me. Then he pushes me back on the bed and runs a hand between my legs. "Shit."

He leans forward to where he knows the condoms are in the nightstand. A rip of foil later and he's on me, his eyes boring into mine as he positions himself between my legs. And then mercilessly slides in hard to the hilt. I don't break eye contact. I can't not watch him.

He fucks me with a desperation I feel deep in my soul. A need to be joined to him like this, to surrender to him, to us. He works my clit, clearly approaching his own peak quickly and not wanting to leave me behind. His other hand touches me everywhere. My face. My neck. My breasts. My stomach.

His touch has a reverence, a depth it's never had. And when we come together, it's forgiveness in flesh, repentance from fear, redemption by love.

28

Open Arms by Journey

West

I wake up in the middle of the night, lying beside Maxi in the dark. And she's snoring so loud that I'm pretty sure it woke me up. Instead of being irritated, it brings a ridiculous grin to my face.

Because I'll fucking take it in a heartbeat. Getting her back is everything. I'll surrender some sleep to her chainsaw-like snores.

I get up and use the bathroom, then stop in the kitchen for a drink of water before heading back to bed. As I climb back in, I realize there's no snoring.

"West?" Maxi's sleepy voice cuts through the dark.

I slide all the way back under the blankets, settling in next to her. "I'm here," I assure her, stroking her hair and wrapping an arm around her.

She wiggles into me and my dick approves, pulsing against what I think is her stomach.

"I dreamed you were singing my song," she mumbles into my chest.

I chuckle. "Really? Or are you just trying to get me to sing it to you now?" I tease.

I feel her smile against my skin. "Will you?"

I run a hand down her hair and take a breath. I was so scared of this moment just yesterday. But now? Not even a little bit.

So I sing to her, losing myself in the story behind the song. It starts off with my life before her, thinking I had it all figured out. Until it moves on to the struggle and frustration of realizing I'm not the man she needs. Finally finishing with the gratitude for learning to forgive, to love both myself and her. Whether she ever loves me again or not.

As I float back to reality, I feel her tears on my chest. I lean in to wipe them away.

"Good tears or bad tears?" I ask after a moment when she doesn't say anything.

"Good," she assures me with a sniff. "You have an incredible voice. Why have I never heard you sing? You know, for real."

She gives me a glare, and I instantly remember what she's referring to: my attempted Maverick moment all those months ago. God, I almost forgot about that. But now's not the time to tease her about it. Now's the time to pony up some of that honesty I promised her.

"Truthfully? My old man relentlessly beat me down anytime I opened my mouth to sing. Kind of takes the fun out of it."

She shakes her head against my arm. "I'm sorry to hear that. You really do have a gift. I had no idea."

"You're just saying that because you love me," I tease. Partially to deflect the praise, having a hard time believing it after all the negative programming. Partially to remind myself that she loves me. Guess I'm not the arrogant bastard I once was, because I feel a little cracked open by all this emotional crap.

She leans up, and I can see the outline of her face above me. "I'm saying that because you have the huskiest, sexiest singing voice I've ever heard. I was touched by your song, West. More than I can even put to words. Nobody has ever written me a song, much less one that beautiful. But your voice?" she takes my hand and brings it between her legs. And she's soaked. "That's what it did to me."

"Fuck," I groan, my lips finding hers in the dark.

Then, between kisses, "You sure know how to compliment a guy."

"And you've sure learned what a woman needs to hear," she replies against my lips. She slips on top of me, her wet core grinding over my dick. And if I thought I was hard before, I'm like granite now.

"Careful," I caution her, not sure how much skin-on-skin I can take before junior explodes.

"I'm done being careful," she murmurs, tilting her hips so I slide into her.

I throw my head back as we groan together. Because holy shit. As her breasts settle on my chest, her lips meet mine, and her hips work me in and out of her … I'm so fucking hers.

I can practically feel the love and trust radiating out of her, and I want to cry like a fucking baby. I never thought I could let someone love me like this. I never thought someone like her could love me like this.

But it's a brand new day. And me? Well, I may not be a brand new West, but I'm sure as fuck going to keep trying. There's no going back, really. Because this woman owns me, body and soul, and fuck if I'm ever going to let her go again.

EPILOGUE

I Melt With You by Modern English

West

Two years later…

"You know, I never thought I'd get to go to a concert without being recognized," I murmur as we take our center seats, a few rows back from the stage. It's not a huge venue but big enough for a sizable crowd.

Maxi smirks up at me. "Don't lie. You miss it," she teases me.

I try not to grin. I swear. But the woman knows me. I don't even need to respond. I simply lean over and kiss her, unwilling to admit it out loud.

But that's not why we're here.

A few minutes later we're joined by James and Jeudi. The women sit next to each other on one side of me, already chatting away as James settles on my other side. We fist bump and exchange greetings.

"So the first concert of our bright new hope," he says, jerking his head toward the stage. "Pretty exciting."

I bob my head. "Sure is." My eyes fall on the row of guitars to one side of the stage.

"You miss it, don't you?" James asks shrewdly.

I throw my hands up and laugh. "Why does everyone keep asking me that?" I tease. And then I sigh. "Yeah. I guess I do. But not as much as you people seem to think. It's nice, helping rising artists the way nobody helped us."

"You mean, not screwing them like we were screwed," James says with a snort.

"Yep, pretty much," I agree. "But you know. It's hard to regret a past that brought you somewhere pretty fucking awesome."

James slaps me on the shoulder. "Aw, look at West, all grown up."

I smirk. "You have no idea."

I'm saved saying any more as the concert starts. And I have to give it to them: Our little rising stars nail that shit. I feel like a proud papa. It's pretty weird.

I mean, don't get me wrong, even though it wasn't my first choice, I still love this gig. But when you go to put out the album you wrote, produced, and recorded all on your own, then your former record label threatens to sue you for using the band name you thought was yours but they had trademarked? That not only puts an end to ever making music with said band again, but it also leaves you severely disillusioned against the music industry.

Who even knew that was a thing? Obviously, not us as kids when we signed the contracts. The knowledge of how much they owned us left me with more than a bad taste in my mouth. It was the straw that broke the camel's back of my music career.

Could I have formed a new band? Possibly. But it seemed like as good a reason as any to retire. It certainly helped me continue my journey toward being a better version of myself. And James had apparently been toying with the idea of going into production and distribution for a while, so it all kind of fell into place and voilà. Instant rock label.

We go out for drinks with James and Jeudi after, then head back to my place, where we pretty much cohabitate anyway, getting home just after midnight. Perfect.

Maxi makes for the bedroom, but I shake my head, grabbing her hand and leading her through the living room, out onto the balcony. It's too dark to see much, but the ocean laps quietly at the shore below us and the hot summer night has barely cooled.

As I turn to face her, she's giving me her "What the fuck are you doing?" look and I have to laugh.

"It's after midnight," I say by way of explanation.

She looks at me blankly. "And?"

"And … it's your birthday?" I prompt.

"Ugh. Don't remind me."

"I still don't get why you hate your birthday so much."

She shrugs. "I just never saw the reason for celebrating. I mean … yay, you managed to stay alive another year? Kinda lame."

I smile. "Then how about we find a way make it special?" I offer, waggling my eyebrows.

She raises one of her own eyebrows at me. "I still don't want to fuck on the balcony, West. Too uncomfortable. Too much potential for witnesses."

I grin and chuckle at her. I'll wear her down on that one someday. "That's not actually what I meant."

Her brows furrow. "Then what?"

"Then this. I tell you how much I love our life together. That I don't miss being a rock star. I don't miss being a fuckup. I don't miss not knowing what I was missing out on. Every day, Maxi. Every fucking day, you make me so goddamn happy. Even when you're busting my chops. Maybe especially then." I wink at her and she rolls her eyes. And god, I fucking love her sass. I draw closer and take her hands in mine. "You're the one who made me want to do better. To be honest. And now, honestly?" I reach into my pocket, fishing out the ring I've been holding onto for weeks. I hold it up between us, pressing my forehead against hers. She gasps when she sees it and looks up at me. "I want to spend the rest of my days with you. There's nothing we can't do together. You're my future, baby. So I just have one question." I stop and look deep into her beautiful hazel eyes. "Max Marshall, will you marry me?"

Maxi's eyes sparkle with tears. "You're so getting fucked on this balcony," she responds, her voice thick.

I laugh. "Is that a yes?"

She nods, throwing her hands over her mouth. "Yes," she cries between her fingers.

I bite into my bottom lip to hold back my own tears, scooping her up and swinging her in a circle. Her arms slip around my neck to hold on, and I cover her mouth with mine. Mine. That's what she is: all mine.

And I thought I'd understood forgiveness and everything after before. But this? This is my redemption. A life with Maxi. Fuck the fame. All that matters is loving her and being loved by her. Forever.

THE END

Want to see what happens between Alexsis and Nils? Get *Giving in to Temptation,* a short story available exclusively by signing up for my newsletter at https://mailchi.mp/melanieasmithauthor/signup!

Curious about Frankie and Julian? She's a human lie detector and he's the muscle sent to scope her out. Find out how they got together in the steamy psychic romantic suspense novel *Everybody Lies.*

Want to talk about the book? Join Melanie A. Smith's Facebook readers group, the Bawdy Bookworms at https://www.facebook.com/groups/137048857974603/

ACKNOWLEDGMENTS

First thanks go to my gallbladder, for giving out and requiring removal. The scheduled surgery lit a fire under my butt to get this book done.

Seriously, though, it forced me to face this book, which I struggled with because it contains some themes that were tough for me personally (as I am sure they are for many). When I was a child, I had a stepfather who was a cocaine addict. It was, perhaps needless to say, extremely tough on our family. So there aren't enough thank yous to my mother for not only making sure we survived, but for being an example of bravery, grit, and setting difficult boundaries.

To my husband, thank you for endlessly discussing plots of books you have no desire to read and generally being ridiculously encouraging and supportive in the face of my frequent whining and exhaustion. Marriage is the best, y'all.

To my alpha reader, Erin, who is just one of the most wonderful human beings on the planet. I'm so thankful she chases after my introverted butt to make sure I know I'm cared for, supported, and appreciated. I appreciate you!

To Jenny, who isn't just my editor, she's a friend I miss dearly and will always wish I lived closer to but still somehow manages to make me feel like there's no distance between us whenever we talk. Love you, babe!

To the book community on social media, whether it be Instagram or Facebook or TikTok, I'm constantly amazed by the authors and readers who are all about support, kindness, and sharing.

To my readers, who finish the stories I start. Thank you. I hope you enjoyed this one.

ABOUT THE AUTHOR

Melanie A. Smith is an award-winning and international best-selling author of steamy contemporary romance fiction. A voracious reader and lifelong writer, Melanie's writing began at a young age with short stories and poetry. Having completed a bachelor of science in electrical engineering at the University of California, Los Angeles, and a master's in business administration at the University of Washington, her writing abilities were mainly utilized for technical documents as a lead engineer for the Boeing Company, where she worked for ten years. After shifting careers to domestic engineering and property management in 2015, she eventually found a balance where she was able to return to writing fiction. Melanie is also a Mensan and enjoys spending time with her family, cooking, and driving with the windows down and the stereo cranked up loud.

facebook.com/MelanieASmithAuthor

twitter.com/MelASmithAuthor

instagram.com/melanieasmithauthor